Christopher felt his own anger building, irrational or not. "Listen, what happened with Carina is history, okay?"

"When you love someone, you love their history, too!" Aisha spat out. "When you marry someone, you want everything—future, present, past."

"Carina has a certain set of problems," Christopher said. "I don't want to discuss it."

"*You don't want to discuss it*!" Aisha shrieked. "Well you'd better start wanting to discuss it, or it's over between us, Christopher."

"Don't give me ultimatums," Christopher said, his voice deadly. "We don't need to discuss it. Carina has nothing to do with you."

A silence more awful than Aisha's shouting filled the room.

"I see," Aisha said. "Is that your final word?"

"Yes."

"Well, then, this is mine. From now on *you* have nothing to do with me, either."

Don't miss any of the books in
Making Out
by Katherine Applegate
from Avon Flare

MAKING OUT #22

Always loving Zoey

KATHERINE APPLEGATE

AN AVON FLARE BOOK

AVON BOOKS, INC.
1350 Avenue of the Americas
New York, New York 10019

Copyright © 1997 by Daniel Weiss Associates, Inc.,
and Katherine Applegate
Published by arrangement with Daniel Weiss Associates, Inc.
Library of Congress Catalog Card Number: 99-95317
ISBN: 0-380-81311-4
www.avonbooks.com/chathamisland

First Avon Flare Printing: March 2000

AVON FLARE TRADEMARK REG. U.S. PAT. OFF. AND IN OTHER COUNTRIES, MARCA
REGISTRADA, HECHO EN U.S.A.

Printed in the U.S.A.

WCD   10   9   8   7   6   5   4   3   2   1

*For my wonderful roommate, Sara Eckel,
who is never above any sort of corniness.*

Always loving Zoey

Zoey

Tonight I really hit
rock bottom or ground
zero or whatever you want
to call it. Some lowlife
stole my purse in the
grocery store (welcome to
Washington, D.C.), and
right now I have seven-
teen cents to my name,
which I found under my
bed in the youth hostel.
Well, I also found nine
hundred Kroner left
behind by some Swedish
person, but who knows
what that's worth.

I was so upset that I
tried to call Lucas right
there in the store, and he
was out at a bar with
Nina. I don't know why
that bothered me, because
if there's anyone who

1

deserves more fun in his life, it's Lucas. I guess I was just being selfish and wanting to hear his voice. Instead I had to call my dad. Not that my dad isn't comforting. After all, my dad is sending me money by Western Union, so I shouldn't complain.

To really round out the evening, I got a ride home with the police officer, who told me that this youth hostel has such a bad reputation that it's known as the Downtown House of Horrors.

Thanks for sharing, Mr. Police Officer. Go choke on your doughnut.

Claire

2:00 a.m. 63 degrees. Wind from the south.

Well, tonight a lot of mysteries were solved—or partially solved.

First, of all, I know what Rayon's blind-date girl looks like. Actually I know what she looks like, sounds like, smells like. I even know what she feels because she told me. She feels that she and Rayon are in love. Rayon told me that he's not in love with Mia (that's her name), but that's not really important, is it? What's important is that he's obviously given Mia enough encouragement for her to think they're in love.

I'm glad he's been staying with Luke on the mainland (the better to visit Mia, my dear). I hope he keeps staying there. I hope he doesn't have the nerve to show up here for a while. Then he can go on tour and make out with a different girl in every town for all I care.

I can't afford to care. I can't afford to look back on these past weeks and wonder just when he's been with Mia, what they've done, what he's told her, how often, etc.

Oh, Aaron. I thought we were perfect for each other. I thought we were so alike. But I would never have done this to you. And that's the difference, I guess.

4

The second mystery I solved tonight was that I now know what was in the photos someone keeps sending me — the ones with happy little sentiments like, I'm Coming to Get You and Just Wait on the back.

The picture is of me. Naked. My back is to the camera, but it's me, all right. The focus is so sharp; you can see the mole on my left shoulder. I remember the night of that photograph. I was getting ready to go out with Aaron. I was happy, humming to myself, twisting up my hair and pinning it, and all along someone was watching me. Watching. Waiting. And photographing me.

Last week I did something stupid: I tore a photograph of a murder

victim out of one of Nina's true-
crime books because it frightened me.
Something about the look in the
girl's eyes (she was still alive
when the picture was taken). I
thought that picture was absolutely
haunting. That was last week. Now I
have this photo to show me what
frightening is all about.

Aisha

When I was growing up—

Wait. That implies that I'm all completely grown up, and that's not true. So let's start over.

When I was younger, I don't think it ever occurred to me to wonder what my future husband's family would be like. I remember when I was about ten, I made up some dumb list of all these qualities I wanted my future husband to have. It was a pretty long list, with things like: tall, drives a red car, never wears sweater vests. I guess my priorities weren't the greatest. But I sure don't remember anything on the list about his family.

I suppose I had some very vague idea that it would be nice if he had a sister because then it would be like me having a sister, which I always wanted. The frustrating thing is that I think Kendra and I could be, if not sisters, at least close. But Christopher won't let it happen.

Why? Why, why, why? It doesn't make any sense. I love the fact that Christopher likes my parents and Kalif. I would be miserable if he didn't like them. So why isn't he happy that I like Kendra and she likes me and we're trying to form some sort of bond? Why go so completely nuts tonight when all she did was show me a picture of him as a teenager? Was it really necessary to chase poor Kendra to the bathroom and yell at her for thirty minutes while I sat alone at the table?

Like I said, it doesn't make any sense. Unless there's something I don't know.

Dear Zoey,

I wish you were here so I could tell you all about how your stupid brother and I just broke up. Of course, Benjamin would never do something as harsh and final as "breaking up." Instead we have "decided not to see each other for a while." Doesn't that sound so much gentler?

Actually it was my decision, too, but only because I knew it was the only decision I could make. I was so unhappy, and I knew something had to change, but —breaking up? (Excuse me, not seeing each

other?) I don't think that's
going to make me tons happier.
In fact, right now it's making
me cry. (That should explain any
smudges on the paper.)

I miss you so much! I
wish you were here so we
could go over every word Benjamin said. We could analyze the
whole breakup until you had
talked me into believing that it
wasn't so bad, that Benjamin
loves me after all, that it will
only make us stronger in the
end. Remember the time you and
I took the bus to the mall,
and halfway there that woman
turned around and said, "You
girls have not stopped for

breath in over twenty minutes. Could you please talk about something other than your boyfriends?" I wish we could take a long bus ride right now so I could tell you everything.

I don't think I'm going to mail this letter after all. I want to tell you everything, and I don't have the time to put everything in a letter. I keep hoping something will happen; that Benjamin will realize what a mistake he made. Then I will send this to you and on the envelope I will write a version of that quote you used to have on your wall:

"Reports of my breakup are greatly exaggerated."

Love,
Nina

LUCAS

Being on this island without Zoey really sucks.

Last night, for example, I went to the Sand Bar with all my friends, and it should have been fun. Instead, everyone got all involved in their own dramas and forgot all about me. I mean, literally forgot. They left while I fell asleep at the bar and woke up with my head resting on some big burly guy's shoulder. Needless to say, he wasn't interested in developing a meaningful relationship.

If Zoey'd been there, that would never have happened. If Zoey had been with me, I would have been all wrapped up in my own drama, my own wonderful

Zoey-filled dRAMA. God, I
miss her so much.

WAS lAst night A pReview
of whAt my life is going to
be like next yeAR when
Zoey's in BeRkeley And I'm
At school with A bunch of
people who ARen't my
fRiends?

ThAt is, if I go to school.
YesteRdAy I wAs—
honestly—looking foR A pApeR
clip, And I hAppened to
see my mom's bAnk stAte-
ment. She must've spent
eveRything on my dAd's
funeRAl. eveRything but A
couple hundRed dollARs, And
thAt won't coveR food And
electRic bills And insuR-
Ance And God knows whAt
otheR expenses. I don't
know. I'm not An Adult. I
don't wAnt to be—I wAnt
to be A college kid. MAybe
theRe's money I don't know
About.

   TheRe'd betteR be,

because otherwise my biggest
problem won't be being without Zoey. It'll be being
here.

One

"I suppose you want to borrow cab fare?" Zoey's roommate, MaryBeth, asked. MaryBeth was the worst part of Washington, D.C., as far as Zoey was concerned. When Zoey had been asked to stay an extra week for a special journalism internship that was awarded to the most outstanding participant in the program, she had accepted. Zoey had never counted on having to spend another week with MaryBeth.

But MaryBeth had counted on being awarded the internship—so her plane ticket wasn't for another week. MaryBeth was taking the week to explore D.C.

"Isn't this great?" she had asked Zoey. "We'll still get to be roomies!"

At this Zoey had merely sighed.

But now she was relieved to have someone to borrow money from. Even if she was the most annoying person in the world.

Zoey nodded. She watched silently while Mary-Beth counted out seven dollars. Zoey's clear, fair skin was even paler than usual, and her dark blond hair was pulled back in a ponytail, accentuating the heart shape of her face.

"You don't mind signing a receipt, do you?" MaryBeth asked.

Zoey shook her head.

MaryBeth wrote, I.O.U. seven dollars! on a scrap of paper and gave it to Zoey. Zoey noticed that MaryBeth had put smiley faces in both the *O* and the point of the exclamation mark. She signed it. She couldn't have cared less. If MaryBeth hadn't agreed to lend her the money, Zoey would have waited until MaryBeth left the room and then she would have smashed MaryBeth's china piggy bank, which had For a Rainy Day written on the side in flowery script. Zoey had had it with MaryBeth. *Who carries a piggy bank around in a suitcase?* she thought. *Get a wallet!*

MaryBeth put the I.O.U. in the piggy bank. Zoey put the money in her jeans pocket and caught a cab to the nearest Western Union center.

She slumped down in the back of the cab, wondering why Lucas hadn't called her. Her anger of the night before had evaporated. She just wanted to hear his voice. And yet he hadn't called. The most likely explanation was that his mother hadn't given him the message. In fact, Zoey found that she couldn't picture Mrs. Cabral actually giving Lucas *any* message. She thought that even if the president called and left a message, Lucas wouldn't learn about it unless the president happened to call back. Later Lucas would say to his mother, *Why didn't you tell me the president called?* and his mother would say, *Do you think I don't have anything better to do than act like your personal secretary?* and Lucas—

"Here we are, miss," the cabdriver said, and Zoey tried to rouse herself. She glanced at the meter. Six dollars. MaryBeth had predicted accurately, of course. Zoey gave the cabdriver all seven and got out.

She went up to the Western Union counter.

"Can I help you?" the clerk asked.

"Envelope for Zoey Passmore," Zoey said. Her voice croaked a little bit. These were the first words she'd spoken all morning.

The clerk flipped through a stack of black-and-yellow envelopes and extracted one. "There you go, Ms. Passmore."

Zoey thanked him and took her envelope outside. She ripped it open standing on the sidewalk in the ovenlike weather. Inside were two hundred dollars in traveler's checks and a letter from her father.

Dear Zoey,

I hope this is enough cash to see you through the rest of your time in Washington. I have also enclosed my Visa number, although you are not, repeat not, to pull a Nina Geiger and max it out. (Yes, word gets around, even to me.)

Sweetheart, you sounded so unhappy on the phone last night that I wonder if Washington is the right place for you right now. I hope you know that no one will think less of you if you decide to come home. I'm not encouraging you to buy a plane ticket, but I imagine the old Visa could withstand a train ticket, and I always found trains to be excellent places to "get your head together," as we used to say in my day.

Best of luck with whatever you decide.

Love,
Dad

Zoey read the letter twice and then groped around in the envelope until she found the scrap of paper with the Visa number on it. She tucked it in her pocket along with the letter. She walked all the way back to the youth hostel, deep in thought.

Nina was sure that Benjamin would call her and tell her that it was all a mistake, a misunderstanding, that he didn't mean it when he said they shouldn't see each other anymore, that he still loved her more than anything. She was so sure he would call that she put the phone by her bed before she went to sleep and woke up at seven A.M., straining her ears for the sound of its ring.

The phone actually did ring at eight-fifteen, and Nina's heart gave a glad leap.

"Hello?"

"Hello, could I please speak to Mr. Geiger?"

"Oh, jeez." One of her dad's stupid businesspeople.

"Excuse me?"

"I'll go get him," Nina said, not bothering to apologize.

The phone rang again at eight-fifty.

"Hello?"

No answer. Just the sound of breathing. *Oh, perfect,* Nina thought. *The crank caller.*

"Could you call back later?" she asked. "We're expecting an important phone call." She hung up.

Some other businessman called at nine, and then Nina dozed a little until the phone rang again.

"Hello?"

"Is Claire there?" It was Aaron.

Nina put her hand over the mouthpiece and bellowed. "Claire!"

19

Claire's footsteps sounded on the stairs. "Who is it?" she called.

"Aaron."

"Tell him I'm not home."

"She's not home," Nina said obediently into the phone.

"Nina, I can *hear* her talking."

She put her hand over the mouthpiece again. "He says he can hear you talking!" she shouted.

"Screw you!" Claire screamed at the top of her lungs.

"Mercy!" said Sarah Mendel, who was walking by with the laundry basket.

"Did he hear that?" Claire shouted.

"Did you—"

"I heard it," Aaron said grimly. "Bye, Nina."

"Bye."

She hung up and stomped to the bathroom to take a shower. When she came back to her room, she found that her CD alarm had gone off and was playing one of the dumb, stupid, obnoxious classical CDs Benjamin had given her. Nina turned it off with a snap.

She stood for a minute, drumming her fingers lightly on the top of the CD player, and then she dug an empty shoe box out of her closet and began throwing all the CDs Benjamin had ever given her into it. If he didn't have the nerve to call her, the simple human courtesy—well, she would take every single reminder of him right over and lay them at his feet. Benjamin would see how cleanly she was excising him from her life.

Mozart, Beethoven, Bach—Nina dumped them in one after the other. Brahms, Debussy, Vivaldi—Nina hesitated. She kind of liked *The Four Seasons*. But principles were at stake here. She threw it on top of the others.

She pulled on a pair of shorts and an old tuxedo shirt that had belonged to her father in the seventies. Her short brown hair had bronze highlights in it from the sun. She ran her fingers through it to fluff it out. A quick pat with a powder puff to hide her freckles, and then some dark lipstick. Her gray eyes stared back at her in the mirror: wide and guileless. She shoved her trademark unlit Lucky Strike between her lips and headed over to Benjamin's.

The Passmores' screen door was open, and Mrs. Passmore was in the kitchen.

"Hello, Nina," she said, stirring a bowl of something. "You're up and about early. Do you want to join us for breakfast?"

"No, thank you," Nina said.

"Are you sure? I'm making waffles."

"I've already had breakfast, thanks anyway," Nina said.

Obviously Benjamin hadn't bothered to tell his mother about the breakup. Was it because he hoped it was temporary, or was it because Nina was such a speck of dust in his life that it wasn't worth discussing? She didn't know.

Nina walked toward Benjamin's room slowly, wondering how many times in her life she'd been in this house, going to Benjamin's room, and Zoey's for years before that. So much history, and now it was all going to be a mess, unless—unless Benjamin was feeling as depressed and regretful as she herself was. Despite herself, Nina's heart swelled with hope. What if Benjamin was sorry about all the things he'd said to her? What if he'd been wishing he could take them back, too? But his pride would keep him from doing that, wouldn't it? He would wait for Nina to make the first move. Maybe—maybe Benjamin had been waiting for *her* to call *him!* Wouldn't that be ironic? If they'd both been waiting for the phone to ring since early this morning?

Nina threw open the door to Benjamin's bedroom. She knew just the look that would shine out of his brown eyes. Pleased, but trying to hide it. Delighted but—

She froze in the doorway.

Benjamin was asleep. He was *sleeping*. He had slept while Nina had fretted and worried and wondered. *The weight of the world had obviously been lifted from his shoulders,* Nina thought, and he was sleeping the sleep of the pure.

She dropped the shoe box of CDs on the floor with a small crash. Benjamin groaned and rolled over.

Nina snapped on the overhead light. She picked up the shoe box and dropped it again, this time onto Benjamin's nightstand. "I'm returning your CDs," she said. It didn't come out at all like she had wanted it to. She wanted to sound firm and regretful. Instead she just sounded shrill.

Benjamin sat up, looking a little puzzled. "Nina?"

"I'm returning your CDs," she said again, still not getting the tone right.

Benjamin looked at the shoe box and frowned. His dark hair was rumpled from sleep. He was wearing only pajama bottoms, and Nina tried not to stare at his chest. "Nina, I gave you those as gifts. I want you to keep them." His voice was gentle and—damn him!— firm and regretful. He looked up at her. "Can't we still be friends?"

"I don't *want* to be friends!" Nina blurted. She

wanted to clap her hand over her mouth. What if Benjamin asked her what she did want to be?

But Benjamin didn't ask her, and when Nina finally summoned the nerve to look him in the eye, she knew that he understood. She knew that *he* knew she had hoped he would either want her back or else have the simple courtesy to leave her alone. Anything would be better than his awful, genuine desire to be *friends*.

Nina could tell by the expression on Benjamin's face that he understood all this—and more. She could have slapped him, if she hadn't loved him so much.

Christopher

FOR A WHOLE YEAR AFTER THE ANNUL-
MENT, I VOWED NOT TO SAY HER NAME. IT
WAS EASIER THAN YOU MIGHT THINK. BUT
WHAT WAS THE POINT? WHAT DID IT
<u>ACCOMPLISH?</u> I KNOW WHAT I'D HOPED IT
WOULD ACCOMPLISH. I'D HOPED THAT BY
NOT MENTIONING HER NAME, I COULD SOME-
HOW WILL CARINA OUT OF EXISTENCE.

BUT THAT'S NOT IT, EITHER, BECAUSE
I DON'T WANT CARINA <u>NOT</u> TO EXIST. I
JUST WANT HER NEVER TO HAVE EXISTED.
AT LEAST NOT IN MY LIFE. I WANT WHAT
HAPPENED TO NEVER HAVE HAPPENED. I KNOW
THAT PEOPLE SAY YOU CAN'T RELIVE THE
PAST. BUT CAN YOU <u>UNLIVE</u> IT? I MEAN,
DOESN'T THE PAST EXIST ONLY BECAUSE
PEOPLE TALK ABOUT IT? SO I BEGAN TO
THINK THAT IF I VOWED NEVER TO TALK
ABOUT CARINA, THEN IT WOULD BE LIKE
IT NEVER HAPPENED.

I KNOW IT DOESN'T MAKE PERFECT
SENSE, BUT THAT'S WHAT I DID. CARINA
IS A PART OF MY LIFE THAT I DO <u>NOT</u>
WISH TO REVISIT. ESPECIALLY SINCE
NOW I HAVE AISHA, AND I DON'T WANT
TO NOT HAVE AISHA ANYMORE. I CAN'T

RISK LOSING HER — I REFUSE TO TAKE
EVEN THE SLIGHTEST CHANCE — ONE MAR-
RIAGE THAT DIDN'T WORK OUT IS MORE
THAN I EVER NEEDED.

Two

Kate woke up, finding it hard to breathe. She couldn't figure out why until she remembered the mattress on top of her. She had a dim memory of crawling between her mattress and box spring the night before, like a mole burrowing underground.

Kate crawled out and stood there, taking deep breaths. The mattress had felt so heavy that she half expected to see a two-dimensional girl in the mirror, something like a paper doll. But she only saw herself: shoulder-length russet hair and the remarkable blue-white skin of a true redhead.

Emotionally she felt like a paper doll, certainly. She saw the suitcase she had packed so haphazardly the night before, but all she could feel was a kind of weary, dull hurt at the way Jake had betrayed her. She remembered the letter from her mother in Jake's coat pocket.

> . . . *I am writing to ask for your help, as Kate is in denial concerning her affliction. She feels she can handle it herself, but I'm sure you'll agree that her place is here with me.* . . .

A small flame of anger burned briefly in her chest. The letter was so manipulative, so self-serving, so twisted, so *typical* of her mother—and Jake had fallen for it! After all, he'd asked for her mother's number, hadn't he?

Kate had to leave North Harbor. She would have to carve out some existence far away from Jake and far away from her mother. But she didn't have the energy.

Her gaze fell on the prescription bottle of antidepressants on her dresser. She was supposed to take a pill five times a day, with food. She had had the prescription filled days ago but hadn't bothered to take a single pill. Now she looked at the bottle with faint interest. She could take a pill now, with some toast and juice, and then go back to bed for a while and take another one when she got up. She would leave North Harbor when she felt stronger.

Kate went down to the kitchen.

Christopher and Kendra shared a grim breakfast of Grape-Nuts. The air between them was electric with tension.

Once Christopher had had a job as the night clerk at a hotel desk, and all he'd done on that job was sit and read thrillers. It wasn't a bad job, although Christopher had gotten a little tired of thrillers. He was especially tired of the way the authors used all those clichés, like *the air was electric with tension* and *the copper taste of fear* and *terror made his mouth turn to cotton* and *he was so scared, he couldn't stop his hands from shaking*. Well, now Christopher knew why those clichés were so popular. It was because they were so accurate.

For example, right this very minute Christopher's mouth was dry, and he could taste pennies, and his hands were shaking so badly, he couldn't pick up his coffee cup. All because of the slight girl with high cheekbones sitting across from him, wearing white shorts and a yellow blouse with a Peter Pan collar and looking the picture of innocence.

Kendra herself seemed oblivious to his turmoil. She stirred her cereal idly. "Do you ever wonder why Grape-Nuts is called Grape-Nuts?" she asked. "I mean, there's really no grapes to speak of. In fact, I can't think of one single food that is *less* grapey or *less* nutty—" She broke off when she saw his expression. "What?"

"You know what."

A look of boredom crossed Kendra's face so plainly that Christopher wanted to strangle her. His whole life was in jeopardy, and Kendra was bored. He struggled to keep his voice calm. "Kendra, I need you to promise me that you won't tell Aisha I was married before."

"I've already promised you a million times."

"It's important."

Kendra carried her bowl to the sink. "Why don't you just tell Aisha the truth? Then you could stop sweating about it constantly, and—hey!" She jumped when Christopher grabbed her shoulders.

He forced himself to merely hold her, not shake her. "I never want to hear you say that again. Do you understand?"

"But Carina is—"

"And I *never* want you to use that name in my presence," Christopher said. His hands tightened. "This is why I need you to promise. You don't know what's at stake. You don't know the half of it."

"You're hurting my shoulders—"

He didn't let go. "Kendra, if you tell Aisha, it will ruin everything, and I will force you to leave town. I can do that. You do know that, right? Now promise me."

"I promise."

Christopher released her, sighing. He didn't like to bully her. He just didn't feel he had any choice.

Kendra rubbed her shoulder showily. "You don't have to be such an ogre," she said. "I can keep your stupid secret."

Christopher said nothing. He sat back down at the table while Kendra gathered her things and set off for the B&B.

"Good-bye," she said.

He nodded.

She was wearing clogs, and he could hear her every footstep on the stairs. He couldn't help thinking that every step took her farther from his control—and nearer to Carina.

Zoey

Pros & Cons of Staying in Washington

Pros

- Mary Beth's socks. They all have little lambs embroidered on them and the monogram MBW. They're hilarious.

- I get to interview lots of famous people.

- I'm getting to explore and enjoy a new city.

- It's the opportunity of a lifetime.

Cons

-Mary Beth's socks. They reflect her personality, which is annoying.

-Every famous politician I've interviewed has put his hand on my leg.

-So far I've been in a bus accident, have had my purse stolen, and am living in the Downtown House of Horrors.

-I miss Lucas.

Speaking of Lucas, a very strange thing happened today. I was taking a nap here at the Downtown House of Horrors, and when I woke up, I had a thought as clear as glass: Get

home to Lucas, I thought.
Now.
  Why would I think
that?

Three

Lucas got home from his day on the fishing boat and his mother greeted him at the door, the ghost of a smile on her wide, plain face. "Why don't you have a shower and I'll fix you something to eat?"

It was so ominous that Lucas thought immediately of the kind of scene in slasher films where some poor slob walks slowly down the hall to certain death.

"Why?" he asked warily.

You know why, a voice in his head whispered. *You know what she's going to tell you.*

"Because I need to have a little talk with you," his mother said. Lucas felt goose bumps pop out all over his skin. Usually his mother barely grunted at him.

He went upstairs and stripped off his dirty lobster-smelling clothes. He sealed them in a plastic bag and put them out in the hall. The smell was so strong that he couldn't put the clothes in his hamper. He would have to wash them tonight.

Lucas stepped into the shower without even waiting for it to heat up and began scrubbing his skin with a special green gel that one of the other fishermen had told him about. It was supposed to

33

be for mechanics, to get rid of car grease, but it did the trick on fish blood and guts and scales, too. Lucas rubbed the gel all over his body and then washed with regular soap. By the time he turned off the water, he didn't smell like a lobster but he thought he kind of looked like one, his skin was so red. He didn't feel clean, exactly; he felt *peeled*.

He finger-combed his unruly blond hair and examined his sunburn in the mirror. He might have to get some zinc oxide for his nose.

Lucas realized that he was delaying going downstairs. He also realized that he couldn't delay forever, so he got dressed and went down. His mother had set the table. Lucas sat down, and she put a dish of spaghetti and meatballs in front of him.

Lucas stared at it. He knew those meatballs. The Passmores had sent them over after the funeral. They were among his favorites, but he didn't think he could eat them now.

"Mom," he said carefully, "what did you want to talk to me about?"

His mother sat down across from him. She pushed her hair behind her ears. Her small face looked very plain and very austere.

"Lucas," she said. "When your aunt Ginger was here, she and I went to every employment agency we could find in Weymouth and Portland, but none of them could find a job for me."

Suddenly Lucas decided to eat one of the meatballs. He had the crazy idea that if he acted normal, everything would be okay. He jabbed a meatball with his fork and popped it into his mouth, whole.

"So?" he said.

His mother looked distressed. "Lucas, don't make things difficult for me. I'm trying to tell you that much as I would like to, I can't afford to send you to college in September. I wish more than anything that things could be different. Life as a fisherman is not what I wanted for you."

The meatball had turned to cardboard on Lucas's tongue. He spit it into his napkin and wiped his mouth. He'd known this was coming. He wasn't an idiot, he was aware of the state of their finances, but hearing it spoken aloud made him feel obstinate and childish. "But there are scholarships and other things," he said stubbornly.

"Lucas, you know that your tuition is not the only stumbling block. What about me? I need the income from the fishing boat."

"But—" Lucas tried to think. Wasn't there some way out? "But we could hire someone to work the boat."

His mother shook her head. "Don't be ridiculous," she said, but her voice wasn't unkind. "You know that wouldn't work."

Of course Lucas knew that wouldn't work. Nobody would work on a boat as small as his father's unless he owned it. And the boat wasn't worth enough to keep them going even if they sold it.

His mother was looking at him, her eyes bright and hot. "I'm going to take a secretarial course," she said, as if she were trying to convince herself as well as him. "You'll only have to work next year, not forever."

Forever. Lucas thought of the carnival psychic telling him that he would never leave the island, that he was chained to it forever.

He pushed away his plate and rested his head in his hands. His vision was blurry, and he wondered why he didn't just put his head down on the table and bawl. He squeezed his hands against his temples.

Forever.

A year wasn't forever. A year was a year. Sometimes a year went by in a happy blur, like this past one. And sometimes a year went by so slowly, you thought you would lose your mind, like the time he'd spent in the Youth Authority.

Forever.

For no particular reason Lucas remembered how his cellmate, a funny, tough guy named Doug, used to mark off the days on the wall using a piece of chalk held between his toes, like a patient in a mental ward.

"Lucas," his mother said softly. "Lucas, I'm so sorry."

He looked up at her and wiped his nose with the back of his hand. "I know," he said.

Claire pushed pieces of poached salmon around on her plate listlessly and watched Nina do the same across the table from her. She was glad that Aaron hadn't had the nerve to come home yet, and even Sarah was off somewhere.

"Girls—" Burke Geiger began.

"Dad, don't," Claire said instantly.

He looked a little taken aback to be cut off before he'd even started. He hesitated and continued, "Well, really, there's no need to act like it's the end of the world."

"Yes, there is," Nina said. "So just pipe down."

"Well, will one of you at least tell me what's going on?"

"No."

Burke hesitated. "How would you girls like to go to the circus this weekend?"

"Dad," Claire said, shaking her head.

"How old do we look to you?" Nina asked. "Besides, the circus didn't even cheer us up when we were little."

"I hate clowns," Claire added.

"Well, what, then?" Burke said. "You've both been so moody. Is it boyfriend trouble? Because you're both too young to be so upset. I mean, there are plenty of other pebbles on the beach."

Nina looked confused. "Pebbles on the beach?"

"He means, other fish in the sea," Claire translated.

Nina groaned. "Dad, please."

Burke held up his hands. "Why are you both acting like I'm an ogre? I just want to know what's wrong. Is—is it some sort of female problem?"

"Oh, ick!" Claire and Nina gave twin cries of disgust and pushed away their plates.

The doorbell rang.

"I'll get it," Claire said instantly, pushing back her chair.

Claire walked down the hall, still holding her dinner napkin, her dark hair swinging against the back of her white blouse. She had slanting dark eyes with thick lashes and rich, full lips. She was strikingly beautiful when she was smiling and even when she wasn't, like tonight. The doorbell rang again as she opened the door.

Aaron was standing on the porch.

"Dad!" Claire called over her shoulder. "The paperboy's here!"

"Claire . . ."

"Oh, that's right, we don't have a paperboy. Sorry." She began shutting the door.

"If you shut it, I'll just open it with my key."

"Why'd you ring in the first place?"

"Because I hoped you would answer."

"Why?"

He leaned one hand against the doorjamb. "You know why."

"Tell me anyway."

"Because I love you."

She wrinkled her nose. "Tell me something else."

"It's true." His eyes were very blue in the twilight.

"Well, tell me something else, anyway."

"Okay. I have a present for you."

"Candy or flowers?"

He laughed. "Nothing that unimaginative." He reached in the pocket of his jeans and handed her a cassette. "It's the band's demo tape."

"Thanks." She took it, careful not to let her fingers touch his. She wished he didn't look so handsome and confident. She wished she didn't want to touch him so much.

"One of the songs is called 'Claire.' "

"You're kidding!" Claire said. "What a coincidence."

"Claire, stop it. . . . You know it's not a coincidence."

"Then it was overly optimistic of you to think I'd still be your girlfriend when the tape came out."

"Oh." He looked away from her, down the street. She looked at his profile. "So . . . you're not my girlfriend anymore?"

She shrugged. "It's pretty immaterial, anyway, isn't it? You're going on tour soon, and you surely won't want a girlfriend for that."

"Why not?"

"Why would you want a girlfriend miles away when every night there'll be pretty groupies throwing their underpants up onstage?"

"Give me a break."

"I don't feel like giving you a break. You better go; the last ferry's in a few minutes."

He smiled painfully. "I was hoping you might want me to stay. I'm getting lonely, staying at Luke's all the time."

"You didn't find it lonely before," Claire said coolly. "In fact, I'm sure you found it nice and close to Mia."

"Claire—"

"Really, Aaron," she said. "I don't want you to stay here, at least for a while. And I don't want to stand here anymore." She didn't tell him that it made her nervous. She knew she was perfectly visible, standing in the backlit doorway at dusk. And what if someone was out there with a camera, waiting to take another photo and mail it to her?

Aaron was looking at her. "Are you okay?"

"Fine." She lifted her chin. "Good-bye."

He hesitated. "Bye." He seemed about to say something more, but Claire shut the door. Then she locked it.

She realized she was still holding something and looked down. It was Aaron's demo tape. She tossed it in the hall wastebasket.

She was halfway up the stairs when she turned back. She fished out the tape and stood on tiptoe to drop the tape inside a large oriental vase. Just in case one day she decided to listen to it.

Four

It was after ten, but Aisha and Nina still sat on the porch swing on the wraparound verandah of the B&B. Aisha wore a short white cotton nightgown with an old gray cardigan over it. She'd just taken a shower, and her dark curly hair was pulled back in a silver clip. She wore no makeup. She didn't need any to define her cheekbones or emphasize the blackness of her eyes and lashes, or add color to her lips. Her eyebrows were arched and expressive.

"So," Nina said, "do you think it was a mistake to take the CDs back?"

"Well, that depends," Aisha said.

"On what?"

"On what you wanted. Did you want an excuse to see him? Or did you really want his CDs gone from your life?" Aisha said.

She wasn't really concentrating. Her fingers toyed endlessly with the snapshot in the pocket of her cardigan. She had studied it so much that she imagined she could feel the contours of the photograph with her fingertips. Such a heartrendingly young Christopher. So open, so happy. Why was he wearing a tux?

"I guess I kind of did want the CDs out of my

40

life," Nina was saying. "I mean, I do kind of feel like a big weight's been lifted off my shoulders whenever I think, I can play any CD I want! It can have people singing! It doesn't have to sound like a piano recital!"

Abruptly Aisha said, "Name an occasion where a person might wear a tux."

Nina brightened. "Is this a quiz? Okay . . . a prom. Now tell me who introduced the potato to Europe."

Aisha frowned. "What does that have to do with anything?"

"I thought we were playing some sort of game," Nina said. "You asked me a question, now I'm asking you a question. Although I have to warn you that if you know the answer, I'm going to write it on a postcard and send it to channel 3's Food Challenge contest."

"No, I wasn't playing a game," Aisha said. "I really want to know."

"Oh, well, in that case, let me think," Nina said. "A wedding?"

Aisha sighed. "Can you think of anything else?"

"Um, a funeral? Easter?"

"Easter?"

"Well, I'm grasping at straws here."

"But *Easter?* Have you ever seen anyone wear a tux on Easter?"

"Yes," Nina said defiantly.

Aisha narrowed her eyes. "Who?"

"A three-year-old boy in church."

Both girls began laughing, and suddenly Aisha was aware of Christopher climbing the porch stairs.

"Hi, Christopher," Nina said.

"Hi." He leaned against the banister. "How are you doing, Nina?"

She groaned and stood up. "Don't ask, unless you have about four hours. But lucky for you I have to go home now."

"Don't let me chase you away."

"No, really," Nina said. "I have to go home and burn some letters or put some pins in a voodoo doll or something equally lovelorn."

Aisha smiled. "Bye. I'll talk to you tomorrow."

"Bye. Bye, Christopher."

Christopher sat down on the swing as Nina went down the porch steps and disappeared into the darkness of the lawn. Aisha turned sideways and rested her feet in his lap.

"What were you and Nina talking about?" Christopher asked casually.

"Oh, her and Benjamin, mostly," Aisha said.

"I mean, right when I got here. It sounded like you were talking about tuxedos."

Aisha didn't look at him. A voice in her head asked, *Why not? Do you think he'll look nervous? Afraid? Deceitful?*

She made her voice light. "No, we were just talking about some quiz show she listened to. Do *you* know who introduced the potato to Europe?"

"Afraid not."

"Me either."

They were quiet for a moment, and then Christopher said, "Eesh, I'm awfully sorry about blowing up at Kendra last night and storming off, leaving you alone."

She shrugged. "It's okay."

"You don't sound like it's okay."

"I'm just tired of having the same conversation," she said. "I keep asking you to be nicer to Kendra or to explain why you can't be, and you keep flying off the handle."

42

"I've told you—"

"Yes, I know. The past is the past, and you want it to stay that way."

Christopher reached over and pushed a strand of hair off her face. "Aisha, you're my future. Can't we just concentrate on that?"

Aisha looked into his face. His dark eyes were steady and imploring. She softened and smiled a little. "Yes," she said gently. "We can concentrate on that."

"Good." He glanced down at her feet in his lap. "Does this mean you want a foot rub?"

"If you don't mind."

He picked up one of her feet and held it in his big warm hands. "Hard day?" His thumbs stroked the sole.

"Brutal," Aisha said. "The B&B is totally full, and Kendra and I have been running around like headless chickens."

"Poor baby," Christopher said. He lifted her foot and gently kissed the instep. Then he kissed her ankle. Then her knee.

"Christopher," Aisha said. "I don't think my parents would like it very much if a guest wandered up and saw this. Actually never mind the guests. If my *parents* saw it, my dad would go get a shotgun."

He didn't stop. "Why is it acceptable for you to sit out here in a nightgown, but not for me to kiss you?"

Aisha laughed. "There's a difference between me sitting here in a relatively demure nightgown and you kissing the inside of my thigh." She swung her legs away from him and sat up, but he was too quick and scooped her into his lap.

43

Aisha sighed and kissed his forehead. She closed her eyes and rested her cheek against his.

If only I could believe it was a funeral, she thought, touching the photograph in her pocket. *Or even Easter.*

In Washington, Zoey stood in front of the room's tiny refrigerator, mixing cucumbers, milk, and oatmeal together. She considered adding some hamburger, just to represent the four food groups, but decided against it.

"What is *that?*" MaryBeth asked.

"A homemade facial," Zoey said.

"Oh—for your wrinkles?"

"I do *not* have wrinkles!"

"Yes, you do."

"I'm seventeen years old."

"Well, what do you call that?"

"What?"

"That?"

Zoey looked in the mirror. "That's not a wrinkle; that's just—just the way my skin moves when I smile. If it didn't move that way, I would be a Barbie doll or a mannequin or something."

"Well, *I* don't have a line there," MaryBeth said.

"I rest my case," Zoey said. It was the highlight of her day.

The Geiger sisters stood in front of the mirror, their faces covered in mud masks. Claire's was green, Nina's orange.

"What should we do while we wait?" Nina asked, looking at their reflections. "Play charades?"

"We don't have to wait," Claire said. "It's already time to peel off your mask. Come here."

Nina stood next to her obediently, and Claire began peeling the orange mask off in big thick strips.

"Ouch!" Nina said. "You're supposed to peel the *mask* off, not my actual face."

"Oh, relax," Claire said. "It can only be an improvement."

"Very funny."

"I thought so," Claire said.

"Keep in mind that I'm going to get to do this to you next," Nina said, wincing.

"No, you're not," Claire said. "Mine is the wash-off kind."

"Oh, that figures," Nina said. "Ask me if I'm surprised. Go on, ask me."

"No," Claire said, scraping at Nina's face with her thumbnail. "It would give you too much pleasure."

Alcohol was oozing out of Lara's pores. She had had eight beers the night before and promised herself that she wouldn't have any tonight. She only drank once a week now. But she could smell last night's beer in her skin.

She didn't wash her face. She liked the smell, although it made her thirsty.

Lucas was putting lemon juice on his face. A fisherman had told him that it would get rid of the lobster smell. Lucas hadn't tried it before this because he thought it sounded vain and girlish. However, for the past two nights he had *dreamed* about lobsters, so he thought he'd better try something.

If he had asked Zoey or Nina or Claire or Aisha or Kate for advice, they would have told him to cut the lemon in half and rub the cut edge against his skin. But he didn't have anyone to show him, so he stabbed a lemon with a fork and squeezed the juice over his face.

His mouth twisted. He grimaced suddenly as the juice worked its way beneath his eyelids. He bent blindly over the sink, splashing water on his eyes, frantically. When he eventually opened them, his eyes were as red as stoplights.

This suited his mood just fine.

Aisha stood in front of the bathroom mirror, putting milk on her face with a cotton ball. She had once had a makeover at the mall and a woman in a lab coat had told her about putting milk on her skin. "After all," the woman said, "your skin is a living organ, and all living things need milk."

This confirmed what Aisha had long suspected: Those lab coats were a fraud, and this woman was not a doctor nor a scientist of any kind. Obviously not all living things needed milk. Plants, for one, didn't need milk. Reptiles. Insects. Birds. Fish. All sorts of things.

On the other hand, Aisha thought, rubbing the milk into her skin, the lab-coated woman didn't have to be a rocket scientist, she just had to help clear up Aisha's complexion.

Benjamin opened the refrigerator. He took out lettuce, tomato, mayonnaise, and ham.

He made himself a sandwich.

Christopher sat in front of the television, watching the Red Sox and eating tortilla chips and guacamole in a messy, satisfying way.

46

Kendra floated by him in a short pink nightgown.

"Go!" Christopher screamed hysterically. "Go, go, go, go, *go!*"

"What a great conversationalist," Kendra said. "A real silver-tongued devil."

Christopher ignored her.

Kendra opened the refrigerator. "Hey," she said, "where's my face pack?"

She and Christopher looked at the bowl of guacamole at the same time.

Nina

So I watched a soap opera today. Zoey told me once that they're good to watch if you have a broken heart. Well, Zoey was wrong. The one that I watched only made me feel worse. There was a couple on there who had recently broken up (it wasn't quite clear why), and they kept meeting accidentally. Every time they met, they would weep and moan and tell each other they couldn't bear to be apart.

Kind of like me and Benjamin this morning. Except for the talking part.

I'm so sorry I went over to see him. It only confirmed my worst fears: Benjamin just seemed <u>relieved</u>. Well, I guess I would be relieved, too, if some girl I was no longer in love with was finally out of my life. Oh, I just had a terrible thought: what if Benjamin has been wanting to break up for a long time? What if he wasn't only relieved but thinking, "Gosh, I should have done that weeks ago"? Oh, I wish that hadn't occurred to me. It's too dreadful to contemplate.

The only good thing—and I

stress the word _only_ — about
going over to Benjamin's this
morning was that at least I
didn't get there in the middle of
breakfast. Can you imagine it? Me
arriving all dewy eyed and there's
Benjamin, shoveling in waffles? I
would say, Benjamin, I love you!
and he would say, Please pass the
syrup.

You'll never see a scene like
that in a soap opera. You
know why? Because the girls
on soaps are all too beautiful.
Soaps never have characters
with bad haircuts or wide
hips or blemishes or boring
love lives. They never have
characters who don't have

someone who is madly in love
with them. There isn't a single soap opera actress who
could play me.

Five

Lucas woke up and smelled his mother's frying bacon downstairs. He didn't remember his talk with his mother at first. He only thought sleepily that it was Sunday morning and he didn't have to take the boat out and he could sleep as late as he wanted—and then it came back to him.

He lay back against his pillow, staring at the ceiling. He was going to have to wake up and stare at the stupid ceiling for the next year and probably the next decade, he thought. Zoey would go off to college, and he would be stuck on this stupid island that, aside from Zoey herself, had never brought him anything but sorrow.

The phone next to his bed rang.

"Hello?"

"Lucas?" It was Zoey.

"Hi, Zo. How are you doing?"

"Terrible," Zoey said.

Join the club, Lucas thought.

"My purse got stolen, and I had to sit in this security cage at the grocery store for, like, two hours," Zoey was saying. "I tried to call you, but you weren't home. Didn't your mom give you the message?"

"No," Lucas said listlessly.

"Where were you, anyway?" Zoey asked.

"Last night?"

"No, the night before."

"Um . . ." Lucas tried to think. Where had he been the night before his mother dropped the bomb? "Oh, I was at the Sand Bar, listening to Aaron's band."

"Oh," Zoey said. She hesitated. "I was so upset. I really—I needed to hear your voice."

"Sorry I wasn't available," Lucas said dryly.

He could hear Zoey's stunned silence.

"Sorry," he said hastily. "I didn't mean that the way it sounded. Was it scary to have your purse stolen?" He tried to concentrate. "You didn't get mugged, did you?"

"No, someone took it from my grocery cart," Zoey said absently. "Lucas, is something wrong?"

Lucas thought about his shattered dreams of college. He thought about his mother and her plans for secretarial school, the fishing boat, the mechanic's gel, the million cuts in his hands from the ropes, the whole sorry mess that was his life. But he didn't tell any of it to Zoey. He didn't feel, right at that moment, as though he could talk about it at all.

"No," he said at last. "Nothing's wrong."

"I miss you," Zoey said uncertainly.

Lucas tried not to sigh. He wished this conversation hadn't worked itself around to *him* comforting Zoey. "I miss you, too."

"Well, listen, I'm supposed to go on a walking tour," Zoey said. "But I could skip it and we could talk—"

"No," Lucas said. "I mean, no, you go ahead.

We'll have plenty of time to talk when you get home."

"Are you sure?"

"Positive."

She hesitated. "I—well, okay. Lucas, I love you."

"I love you, too."

"Good-bye."

"Bye."

Lucas was thoughtful for a moment, then quickly dialed a number.

"Hello?"

"Nina? It's Lucas."

"What's wrong?" she asked.

"What do you mean?"

"What do you mean, 'What do I mean?' Something's the matter; I can hear it in your voice."

He smiled faintly. "You could tell that just from me saying, *Hi, it's Lucas?*"

"Uh-huh." It sounded like she was eating something. "So, are you going to tell me what it is?"

He hesitated. "Not now."

"Sure?"

"Yeah."

"Okay . . . so ask me how I am."

"Sorry. How are you, Nina?"

"Let me put it this way, if I had a hollow tooth filled with cyanide, I'd knock it out about now."

"Why?" Lucas asked, concerned. "Did something happen between you and Benjamin at the Sand Bar? Where did you go, anyway?"

"I'll tell you later," Nina said, whispering.

"Okay," Lucas said. "I tried to call you all yesterday, but I kept getting a recording saying your phone was out of order."

"It was off the hook," Nina said. "We got another crank call, and Claire threw the basement phone across the room."

"Why didn't you just hang it back up?"

"Because she didn't tell anyone she'd thrown the phone, and we didn't hear it beeping because it's in the basement. *And* my dad called a telephone repairman," Nina said, sounding a little overheated. "But since Claire isn't here, my dad told me to stick around, and so I had to be the one to get the repair guy's lecture about wasting his time and it being Sunday and all. He's still here, in fact. Right now he's eating pancakes and brown sugar and telling Janelle his life story."

"Is he finished?" Lucas asked.

"Are you kidding? He's only up to about 1958, when he joined the Navy."

Lucas laughed and then stopped suddenly. Had he really laughed on this, one of the worst days of his life? "No, I mean, is he finished repairing the phone?"

"Oh, sure, all he had to do was hang it up. A monkey could have done that. Those are his words, not mine."

"Well, then, are you free to go somewhere? For a walk or something?"

"Oh, my God," said Nina. "I thought you'd never ask."

Six

Christopher eased Aisha's bedroom window open, hoping that Mr. Gray wouldn't mistake him for a prowler and shoot him. Christopher doubted that there were many prowlers out and about at ten-thirty in the morning, and even fewer carrying breakfast trays, but you never knew. In fact, he thought it was more probable that Mr. Gray would recognize him for what he was—an eager young guy climbing into his daughter's room—and shoot him, telling the police he *thought* it was a prowler.

Christopher smiled to himself at the thought. The idea of gentle, bookish Mr. Gray getting a shotgun seemed pretty unlikely.

He threw a leg over the windowsill, keeping the breakfast tray carefully balanced, and slipped inside.

Aisha was still asleep, curled up like a little girl, her hands clasped under her cheek.

Christopher sat on the edge of the bed, the tray on his knees. He picked up one of the plates and waved it gently under her nose. "Aisha . . . wake up . . . smell the cinnamon bun?"

Her eyelids fluttered.

"That's a good girl . . . open your eyes . . . come on, now."

Aisha's eyes flew open, she looked at him for a panicky minute, and then she groaned and flopped back against the pillows with her arm thrown over her eyes.

"You know, my dad would kill you if he knew you sneaked in here like this."

Christopher touched her lips with the cinnamon bun and she took a bite, still with her eyes covered. "Could we spend less time talking about your dad killing me?" he said. "He might overhear and get ideas."

Aisha laughed. "He already has ideas, believe me." She lifted her arm and peered at him. "Can I have some more cinnamon bun?"

Christopher handed it to her. "And there's eggs and bacon and toast and strawberry jam."

She looked at the tray and then at him. "What did I do to deserve this?"

Christopher smiled. "Well, didn't you tell me yesterday that you'd been running around like a headless chicken, waiting on other people? I thought you might like someone to wait on you."

"Oh, Christopher," Aisha said. "You work hard enough yourself. I don't need you to wait on me." Her dark eyes were worried.

He picked up one of her hands. "I like to wait on you," he said softly. "It makes me happy."

She glanced down at the tray and laughed suddenly. "Did you just walk across town carrying that? Complete with the rose in a bud vase?"

He nodded.

Aisha rolled her eyes. "What a nut. I bet everyone knew exactly where you were going, too."

Christopher picked up the goblet of orange juice from the tray and took a sip. "I'm sure everyone knew," he agreed. "They all thought it was—" He stopped.

"Christopher?" Aisha said.

He couldn't answer her. He'd been about to tease her and say, *They all thought it was our post-make-out munchies,* but now he couldn't form any words at all. He opened his mouth, but no sound came out.

His wedding portrait was propped up on Aisha's nightstand.

He stared at it idiotically. He had thought the picture had been ruined in his blowup with Kendra at the Sand Bar. Although he saw Kendra give the picture to Aisha—he and his sister had gotten into a huge fight over it, after all—he had assumed that it had been swept up by a waitress and thrown in the trash, or that it was so covered with sticky Coke as to be unrecognizable. But no, there he was, grinning like a jerk in his tux, with his stupid hair looking like it should be a cartoon balloon with words in it.

"Christopher?" Aisha said again.

His mind was swaying. *She's suspicious,* he thought. *She was talking about tuxedos with Nina last night. She doesn't just remember the picture, she* has *the picture.* What was he going to tell her? What could he possibly say?

"Christopher?"

His paralysis broke. He forced himself to chuckle, still looking at the picture. "Where on earth did you get that?"

There was a sharp line between Aisha's eyebrows. "Kendra gave it to me."

"Oh, so this is the picture she showed you night before last?"

"Yes, I thought you saw it."

"No, no," Christopher lied. He made himself pick up the picture. "I just knew she showed you a picture. I didn't know of what. I thought she'd given you something seedier looking, a picture of our house or neighborhood or something."

"Why—why are you wearing a tuxedo?" Aisha asked.

"I was at a dance."

"But you said your school didn't have proms."

"It didn't. It was a church dance." The lie came to him as easily as if he'd sat up all night planning it. "See, there's stained glass in the background."

Aisha took the picture. "Oh, yes, I see," she said. Her voice was full of relief.

"It wasn't a very fun dance," Christopher said. "They didn't have very good music since it was sponsored by the church. We had to dance to all these dumb Christian-rock songs." He didn't know where his mind was digging up all these false details; he was just glad to have them.

He looked at Aisha and then was sorry he had. Her face was shining with trust. She looked ready to promise him anything. He could read in her eyes that she believed him, that she had just brushed a thousand doubts from her mind.

She glanced at the picture again. "You look happy, though," she said.

"Yes," Christopher said. "I do. I suppose I was."

Lucas met Nina on the corner of Dock Street and Leeward Drive. She was wearing jeans and an old navy blue moth-eaten sweater with Cornell written above the breast pocket.

"Hi," Lucas said. "Is that your dad's sweater?"

"My grandpa's," Nina said, looking pleased. "Do you like it?"

"Yes," Lucas said. He did like it, on her.

They began walking out of town, toward the beach. *It's going to rain,* Lucas thought, looking at the bank of dark clouds gathering.

"You go first," Nina said. Her nose and eyelids were faintly pink, and the skin on her cheeks had an odd dappled look. He wondered if she had a cold, but then he realized she'd been crying. What had happened, anyway? It must have to do with Benjamin. They must've had a fight, a big one.

"Okay," he said. "I don't mind going first." And he told her about his conversation with his mother.

When he finished, she looked stricken. "Oh, Lucas," she said, rubbing her cheeks. "How terrible. Have you written the university for a deferment?"

"A what?"

"A deferment," Nina said. "If you write them and explain about your dad dying and your family's financial situation, they'll grant you a deferment, which means you won't have to reapply next year. You can just go a year later."

Lucas almost said that he thought he wouldn't be going to college next September, either, but then he stopped. Who knew? Maybe he would. It certainly wouldn't hurt to have a deferment. It would be something to look forward to.

"And there might be night classes offered in Portland," Nina said. "We'll call and find out."

Lucas glanced at her and wanted to laugh. She looked like a miniature Burke Geiger, brow furrowed, working out a solution. And suddenly he realized that he felt much better. Nina had helped him. She had looked at the situation and not let pity

60

overwhelm her. She had been practical and kind, and thought of things he had overlooked.

Lucas felt a small part of his burden slip from his shoulders to hers, and he marveled that out of everyone he knew—his mother, his relatives, Zoey, her family, his friends—that it should be this girl whom he was hardly even friends with, this girl in the unraveling sweater, who should help him most of all.

They had reached the beach. The sea was rough and gray, and dark clouds were accumulating ominously, but neither of them noticed. They didn't feel the wind or the sand as it drove into their skin and eyes.

"So what happened with you and Benjamin?" Lucas asked.

"Oh, nothing important," Nina said absently. She still looked like Burke. Lucas guessed her mind was still wrestling with his college problem.

"It must be important," he said softly. "Did you have a fight?"

"You might say that." Nina looked up at him. Her eyes were as gray as the thunderclouds. "We broke up."

"You broke up?" Lucas said incredulously. "For good?"

"It sure seems that way," Nina said, crossing her arms and hugging her elbows. "It's definitely over as far as Benjamin is concerned. I went over there yesterday, and you would have thought I was there to read the gas meter, for all the personal attention he gave me."

"But—why?" Lucas asked. "Why did you break up?"

"I don't know!" Nina said, exasperated. "Ask

Benjamin; it was his idea. Well, that's not fair, I guess it was partly my idea, too. I just couldn't go on, the way things were."

"What things?"

"Oh, well, you know how Benjamin's been ever since he got his sight back," Nina said bitterly. "He wants to do everything right now, right away. That doesn't leave much time for some boring hometown girl who's not even old enough to be going off to college or anything interesting."

"Nina—" Lucas hesitated. He wished he could do the same for Nina that she'd done for him. He wished he could think of some positive action to take. "I'm so sorry," he said at last. It sounded lame, even to him.

"Oh, don't be," Nina said, hugging herself tighter. "I should have seen it coming a long time ago. It probably should have *happened* a long time ago. He hasn't paid me an ounce of attention in weeks, except to be jealous of you."

Lucas's eyebrows shot up. "Jealous of me?"

"Oh, that was *so* stupid." Nina rolled her eyes. "I could hardly even believe it. Remember when you took me out on the lobster boat? I went to get lunch, and Benjamin thought I was ordering a ham sandwich especially for you, so he sort of flew off the handle." She looked miserable, concentrating on her feet and kicking up little sprays of sand. "But I mean, if he'd bothered to think about it for even a second, he wouldn't have taken it seriously. It's not like he doesn't *know* that you would never be interested in someone like me."

Lucas stopped walking. "What do you mean, someone like you?" he asked.

Nina bit her lip, looking embarrassed. "Oh, just

that, you know, you've always gone out with girls like Zoey or Claire, who are . . . you know, beautiful. And not with girls like me, who have, you know"—there was a pause—"something wrong with them."

"Nina," Lucas said, shocked. "There is nothing wrong with you."

Her large gray eyes filled with tears. "Then why—"

"What?"

She gestured inarticulately. "Then why doesn't anybody *love* me?"

Lucas stood there, shocked. "Nina—"

"You don't *know* what it's *like* to live with *Claire*," Nina spat out. "Guys always want Claire—and she is *such* a . . ." Nina looked up at him through her tears. "Nobody even *looks* at me—because she's beautiful, and I'm not. Do you think it's a coincidence that Benjamin got his sight back and then dropped me? Because I don't."

"Nina, stop it." Lucas put a hand on her shoulder. "Please. Just stop it." He felt sick, standing there. He knew that what she was saying wasn't true, but he was never good with words, and he didn't trust himself now.

"Nina—you know that—what you're saying"—he fumbled lamely—"isn't true. It isn't fair. Benjamin does care about you, but—this isn't an easy time for him. And Nina—you *are* beautiful—"

"No, I'm not."

"You're beautiful where it counts."

"But why doesn't anybody love me?" she demanded.

"Nina—" Lucas looked exasperated. "*Everybody* loves you. Zoey loves you. Burke loves you.

63

Benjamin may have broken up with you, but he still *loves* you. *I* love you—" He broke off, surprised at himself. But that didn't make what he had said any less true.

Nina rubbed her nose with the back of her hand. "You do?"

Lucas looked at her upturned face. Her lips were raspberry colored and tender looking, probably from crying and now the wind.

A wave of sympathy washed over Lucas. Nina was so fragile. At that moment he would have done anything to comfort her. But what could he say? If only he were good with words, but Lucas was always more comfortable with action. If only he could *do* something for her . . .

"Really? You do?" Nina asked, and Lucas lowered his head and kissed her.

It was a slow, gentle kiss, and at first Lucas wasn't quite sure why he'd done it. Maybe just because her lips looked so bruised and vulnerable. Their noses bumped, and he turned his head slightly, his lips never leaving hers.

He felt her arm slip lightly, tentatively, around his neck, and he pulled her closer to him, sheltering her from the wind with his body. His hands were on her shoulder blades, which he could feel clearly even through her sweater. They felt as delicate and brittle as wishbones.

And he realized something else as he held her and kissed her and she kissed him back. Nina was trembling.

Seven

I'm being unfair to Lucas, Zoey thought suddenly.

She was on a walking tour of the monuments that she had signed up for spontaneously. Zoey thought she would melt in this hellish D.C. weather. She could feel the heat of the pavement right through the soles of her espadrilles. The walking-tour guide had a big bandage on his forehead where he'd hit his head on the sidewalk after fainting in the heat yesterday. Zoey wasn't paying much attention to him.

She was thinking about Lucas. She cringed when she thought of how demanding and selfish she must've sounded this morning. She hadn't meant to imply that he should wait by the phone in case she needed him. Poor Lucas, he had to slave away on his father's fishing boat six days a week. The least she could do was cut him some slack. Besides, all he'd done was go to the Sand Bar with Nina and the gang. And wouldn't she rather have him go out with her best friend than some unknown bombshell?

The walking tour moved on, and Zoey dutifully trooped along. She gathered her hair into a ponytail and secured it there with the twist tie from an old sandwich wrapper in her pocket. She supposed that she looked less than glamorous, but she couldn't have cared less. She was too hot.

The only good thing to come from this trip, Zoey thought, *is that at least Nina and Lucas seem to be friends now. That's good. I wanted that.*

She frowned, though, as she thought of how unhappy Lucas had sounded on the phone. He'd sounded so depressed.

Zoey put her hand in her pocket and touched the letter from her father. It was damp and curling at the edges from the humidity.

The guide pushed his sweaty hair off his forehead. "Does anyone have any questions?"

Zoey hesitated and then raised her hand.

"Yes?"

Zoey swallowed. Her hand tightened on the letter. "Can you direct me to the train station?" she asked.

When Lara arrived at the Passmores', they were all in the backyard, playing badminton and having some sort of argument. At least Lara thought it was an argument. With the Passmores it was hard to tell whether they were arguing or joking.

"That is not fair play," Benjamin said, rubbing his forehead.

"Of course it is," Mrs. Passmore answered indignantly. "You would have done the same to me if you had the chance."

"No, I wouldn't," Benjamin said. "I wouldn't slam the birdie into my own son's forehead. Look, we're playing two against one; the least you can do is not try to disfigure me with your ruthless overhand."

Mr. Passmore looked up and saw her. "Well, Lara's here," he said. "So we can start over."

They all turned to look at her. "Hi," Lara said awkwardly.

"Do you know how to play badminton?" Mr. Passmore asked.

Lara shook her head, wishing she hadn't come. She hated being forced to play games. She might have known something like this would happen when Mr. Passmore invited her over for a barbecue. "I'm not very coordinated," she said hesitatingly.

"Good," Benjamin said. "Because if you were, you'd have an unfair advantage over the rest of us, and we'd make you go play volleyball with the Prestons next door. You want to be on my team?"

"I guess," Lara said sullenly. She wondered if she could make up some excuse and escape.

"Okay, basically it's like tennis, except slower," Mr. Passmore said to Lara, handing her a racket. "Which is good because we're all too lazy to dart around after the birdie."

"Except my mother, who uses it as a way to work out her aggression," Benjamin said helpfully. "Come on, let's play before it rains."

Lara was relieved to find that badminton was an easy game and that none of the Passmores gave her any advice. And they didn't praise every shot in a condescending way. They just let her play while they kept up the steady stream of conversation that always surrounded them.

"Did you see that woman in the restaurant last night throw a glass of water at her husband?"

"Does anyone know what movie's playing in Weymouth?"

"Where did Nina Geiger go for that haircut?"

"Did you read in the paper about the burglary?"

"What should we do on the Fourth of July?"

On and on they went, while the birdie bounced back and forth against their rackets with a pleasant *ponk*. Lara was almost sorry when Mrs. Passmore said, "Let's have something to eat."

She dropped her racket and went into the house, reappearing almost immediately with a tray of strawberries and four glasses of champagne. She set the tray on a garden table.

Mr. Passmore handed glasses to everyone. "Well," he said, raising his own glass. "To Lara's first badminton game."

Lara hesitated. Mr. Passmore saw. "It's nonalcoholic champagne," he said.

Did they do that for me? Lara wondered. *To show me how supportive and accepting they are? How creepy.*

Benjamin must have seen something in her expression. "We can't have real champagne," he said. "Or else Dad gets loopy."

"Yep," Mr. Passmore agreed. "One glass of champagne, and it's lamp-shade-on-the-head time."

And they were off talking about something else, and Lara stopped wondering whether the nonalcoholic champagne was for her benefit or not. They were only halfway through the strawberries when they felt the first drops of rain.

"Let's move to the porch," Mr. Passmore said.

"We better pick up the rackets," Mrs. Passmore replied.

"I'll do it." Mr. Passmore trotted around the backyard while Lara helped Benjamin and Mrs. Passmore pick up the glasses.

"Hi!" Mr. Passmore said to someone in the neighboring yard. He wandered over to the edge of the yard. "Yeah, it looks like a pretty bad storm. . . .

Sure . . . Tuesday? We'd love to. . . . Why don't you come over for dinner and then we'll go . . ."

Lara felt the same sudden isolation she felt whenever she heard the Passmores making plans. Lara had such a tiny part in their lives. She wouldn't be having dinner with them on Tuesday or any other night, for that matter.

Why do you care? she asked herself.

They barely made it to the porch by the time the storm struck. Lara was surprised that they didn't all rush around shutting the windows. Sometimes the Passmores were more laid back than she gave them credit for.

Mr. Passmore went into the kitchen this time and brought back a tray of barbecued chicken. He set it on a low table between two couches, and they all gathered around, grabbing pieces and eating with their fingers. The rain drummed steadily on the roof.

"There was a message on the machine from Zoey," Mr. Passmore said. "I guess we didn't hear the phone out in the backyard."

Thank God for small favors, Lara thought sourly.

"What'd she say?" Benjamin asked.

"Nothing much," Mr. Passmore answered. "Just that she would call back later."

"I wonder if the police have found her purse," Mrs. Passmore said.

"Zoey lost her purse?" Lara asked, just for something to say.

"Someone stole it out of her shopping cart," Mrs. Passmore explained.

Well, how dumb can you be? Lara thought. *Why didn't she have it over her shoulder? I bet she cried like a big baby.*

"She was terribly upset," Mr. Passmore said.

"I bet," Lara said. "I mean, I bet it was very upsetting."

The chicken and the rain were comforting her. She felt drowsy and relaxed. She watched Mr. Passmore eating a drumstick. It was his fourth. He was eating with his eyes closed in a kind of dreamy state of pleasure. He might be kind of a dork, Lara thought, but she liked the way he devoted himself so completely to basics, like eating.

Mr. Passmore opened his eyes. "What are you thinking?" he asked Lara. He had grease on his chin.

"I'd like to paint your picture," Lara said, surprising herself.

Nina wasn't sure why she was trembling, but it had started as soon as Lucas kissed her, and she couldn't seem to make herself stop. She leaned against Lucas on the windy beach, pressing closer to him, her arms locked around his neck, standing on tiptoe to press her mouth more firmly against his.

She thought that if she could just get close enough to Lucas, just lose herself in Lucas, then she would stop shaking and he would make her feel all right—

Thunder broke over their heads with a sudden crash, and Lucas jumped. He ripped her arms from around his neck and stood there, breathing heavily, holding her hands so hard, she thought he would crush them.

He looks like he wants to shake me, Nina thought dizzily.

Abruptly he dropped her hands. "God," he said. "Zoey."

For a second Nina thought he was calling her by Zoey's name. Then she realized that he meant something else.

I am a horrible person, she thought sickly.

The rain burst upon them, falling as heavily as sand out of a dump truck. It fell so thickly that Nina could no longer see the expression on Lucas's face.

He grabbed her hand, more gently this time. "Come on," he said loudly, above the sound of rain on the ocean. "I'd better get you home."

Nina followed him, silently, meekly. He didn't let go of her hand, pulling her along the way he might keep track of a younger sister on a crowded street.

They had to bend forward against the wind, and conversation was impossible, which Nina supposed was just as well. They had both been so soaked in the first few moments of the storm that Nina barely felt the rain now. Her grandfather's sweater was a sodden mass, and her sneakers squished with every step. She knew her hair had probably slicked down into a dumb-looking dark little elf's cap.

It doesn't matter what I look like, she told herself. *I'm sure all he can see is Zoey, even when he looks at me.* Lucas was taking her home now. He would walk her to her door and leave her alone with this horrible thing they'd done.

She glanced at Lucas out of the corner of her eye. The rain had made his T-shirt almost transparent, and she could see where it stuck to the muscles of his chest. His hair was curling into water-dark, dripping ringlets, and his profile looked set and unhappy. Nina looked away.

She concentrated on the squish, squish of her tennis shoes and let Lucas pull her along. Water ran off her hair and blurred her vision.

Lucas stopped at the end of Nina's street.

71

"Can you make it from here?" he shouted. "I have to go secure the boat."

Nina nodded. She supposed she was just as glad that no one would see him walk her to the door. *God, we're acting like criminals already,* she thought.

Lucas squeezed her hand. "We need to talk," he said. "Later." And then he was gone, an indistinct shape in the pouring rain.

Nina took off her sneakers and walked the rest of the way home, her bare toes squelching in the mud on the sidewalk. She didn't really think that she and Lucas would talk later. What would be the point, really? Lucas's first thought had been of Zoey. Nina, in those few moments when Lucas had pulled her tight against him, hadn't thought of Zoey at all.

Eight

Claire stared out the window at the storm with longing, the way a golfer or tennis player might look at a bright sunny afternoon. Claire wanted to be outside. She wanted to sit on her widow's walk and feel the heavy sooty bellies of the clouds pressing down on her while the wind picked up speed. Her pores opened up just thinking about it.

But Claire didn't like to sit on her widow's walk these days. Who knew who might be out there with a camera? You never knew. No, Claire didn't want to sit outside and watch the storm.

But the weather made her restless, and she paced around the kitchen, making Janelle nervous.

"Do you want something?" Janelle said. "I'm making chocolate chip cookies, but they won't be ready for a few minutes."

"Why are you making cookies?" Claire said.

"To cheer Nina up."

Claire smiled wryly. "Don't I need cheering up, too?"

"No," Janelle said, shaking her head. "Not in the same way."

"Why not?"

"Because you never *needed* anyone, not even when you were a little girl," Janelle said. "Besides,

Aaron's been calling and coming around, but have you seen hide nor hair of Benjamin?"

Claire sighed. "Unfortunately, no."

Janelle gave Claire a smile. "That's why Nina needs cheering up more than you do. Now, why don't you go watch the storm like you're dying to do, and I'll call you when the cookies are ready."

Claire left the kitchen. The storm was still raging outside. Well, she could watch it from her bedroom window. She didn't have to go out in it. She climbed the stairs.

But it wasn't the same, and soon she found herself pacing her room in the same manner she had paced the kitchen. Finally she settled at her desk and turned on her computer.

She needed to put her thoughts in writing, and she didn't want to write them in her diary. *Just in case,* and this was an ugly thought, *I ever need to print this out and show it to someone. Like the police.*

> We now have an unlisted phone number. Dad said that it would be a lot simpler than throwing phones and things like that. He asked me why I hadn't told him about the phone calls if they bothered me so much. Well, that's a good question, isn't it? And why don't I tell him about the photographs? And the feeling that someone is watching me and getting closer every minute?
>
> I guess it's what Janelle just said: I've never needed anyone. And I don't want everyone looking at me in that weird way and saying stuff behind my back: "Yes, that's Claire Geiger.

Haven't you heard? She hardly ever goes out anymore. Yes, she's very pretty. Apparently someone else thought so, too."

I wish I could believe that it was some random guy who saw me sashaying along Main Street and decided I was just too pretty to pass up. I wish I could believe that. But I can't stop thinking that it's someone I know, someone I've hurt.

I've been thinking about going to the police. I would have to plan what to say, give them a list of suspects. It would be funny if it weren't so pathetic. I'm being stalked, but the worst part is that it could be any one of dozens of people.

The McRoyans Obviously they must still hate me and blame me for Wade's death. That's not the kind of thing you ever get over.

Jake Jake, I'm sure, also hates me and blames me for Wade's death, plus all the bad relationship things that have gone on between us.

Mrs. Cabral She hates me because I wasted two years of Lucas's life and tainted the family name.

Lucas I'm sure he hates me even more, given that it was his two years that got wasted.

Aaron Aaron doesn't hate me, but it did occur to me that he wouldn't be above frightening me. Why? Well, that's harder to answer. Maybe it started as a joke and

"Claire!" Janelle shouted. "Do you want some cookies?"

"I'll be right down," Claire called. She pushed back her chair and went down the stairs.

Janelle had left a plate of cookies and a glass of milk on the first landing. Claire took a bite of one of the cookies and closed her eyes. Janelle was probably the best cook in the world. The cookies *would* cheer Claire up, even if they had been meant for Nina.

She had begun carrying the plate and glass back up the stairs when she heard a strange beeping noise. *Beep. Beep beep. Beep.*

Claire frowned. Was it coming from her room?

Beep. Beep beep beep beep.

She hurried up the stairs and rounded the corner into her room. *Beep. Beep. Beep.* It was coming from her computer. Hastily she set down the plate and glass and bent to study the screen.

Beep. Beep. Beep.

Claire's forehead grew clammy, and her hands turned to ice.

Beep.

The cursor was moving backward through Claire's diary entry, deleting her words letter by letter. And every time a letter disappeared, it beeped.

Beep.

Numbly Claire pressed the space bar. The cursor didn't pause. It continued its backward journey, eating up all her words. She pressed the enter key, the insert key, but it was no use. The cursor worked its way back to the top of the page. Then it stopped. Everything Claire had written about the stalker was gone.

Claire stared at the screen. Her eyes were huge.

The cursor had stopped beeping. It flashed slowly in place, cold and green and malevolent. Claire thought inanely that it looked like a glowing green eye, waiting. But waiting for what?

The cursor flashed again, and then it moved. A *C* appeared on the screen. And then an *L*. Claire couldn't take her eyes off it. *A,* spelled the cursor. Claire's hands crept up to rub her cold cheeks. *I . . . R . . . E . . .*

The storm struck the house suddenly, and the electricity dimmed for a moment. The cursor blinked off the screen with an audible pop.

Claire bit back a scream.

"Aisha, why don't you take a break for an hour or so?" Mrs. Gray said innocently, hunting for her shopping list in her purse.

Aisha narrowed her eyes. "Why are you being so nice? What horrible thing do you have planned for tomorrow?"

"Dear, that's no way to talk; I'm always nice to you."

"I repeat, what horrible thing do you have planned for tomorrow?"

Mrs. Gray sighed. "I need you and Kendra to clean out the attic."

Aisha groaned. "Mom, what are you going to do when I leave for college? Close the B&B? Or are you going to actually make Kalif get off his lazy butt?"

Mrs. Gray found her shopping list and put on her raincoat. "I would love to have Kalif do more," she said. "But he's so incompetent."

"That's an act, Mom," Aisha said. "Precisely so you *don't* give him more responsibility. Like the time you asked him to drive the golf cart over to the grocery store."

"What about that time?" Mrs. Gray asked. "He ran over Mr. Peterson's foot. If that's not incompetence, I don't know what it is."

Aisha rolled her eyes. "He's out in the yard every day, driving that cart perfectly."

"In circles," Mrs. Gray said. "All he does are wheelies."

"Brodies," Aisha corrected automatically. "Anyway, I can see this is totally pointless and you're going to keep letting Kalif goof off."

Mrs. Gray smiled tolerantly. "Good-bye, dear. I'll be gone for a couple of hours, but Kendra is in the kitchen, polishing the silver. She can help anyone who needs it. You go on and take a nap or something." She took her umbrella and went out the door.

Aisha listened to the rain drumming on the windows like handfuls of gravel and decided to take a nice hot bath. She went up to her parents' bathroom because it had a huge, seventy-gallon bathtub.

Aisha turned on the taps and added bath salts. She began undressing, remembering to lock the door first. That was another bad thing about living in a B&B—guests were likely to burst into a room at any time of the day or night. Once in the middle of the night Aisha had gone down to the kitchen for a snack, and when she got back, Mr. Crenshaw was barfing into her bedroom wastebasket. (He later claimed that he thought her bedroom was the bathroom; her wastebasket, the toilet. Aisha supposed it could have been worse.)

She pinned up her hair and examined her body in the mirror. She had to admit that running up and down the stairs five thousand times a day was good for her figure. Her thighs were slim and firm, and when she turned sideways, she could see the outline of her quadriceps.

Still, Aisha groaned as she lowered herself into the steaming water. She'd rather work out at the gym like a normal person. She rested her head against the lip of the tub. The bathtub was so huge that her entire body was underwater, without her knees poking out. She closed her eyes, and immediately the doorbell rang.

Her eyes flew open, and then she remembered Kendra. Kendra could answer the door. She closed her eyes again.

"Oh, hi."

Kendra's voice was so distinct, so loud that Aisha sprang halfway out of the tub, heart hammering, before she realized she was still alone in the bathroom.

"Is Aisha here?"

That was Christopher's voice. Aisha peered over the edge of the tub at the metal grating on the floor. Their voices were coming through the heating vent.

She lowered herself back into the tub and was immediately swept up in a horrible paranoid suspicion that she and Christopher might have made out in the exact spot where he was now standing with Kendra. And if her parents were in the bathroom— she didn't even want to think about it.

". . . taking a nap or something," Kendra was saying. "You can go and find her."

"No, that's okay. I just have a minute, anyway."

"If you just had a minute, why'd you come over?"

"Well—"

Kendra's voice was full of irritation. "Look,

Christopher, I don't need you popping over every two seconds to see if I've dropped the bomb yet."

Bomb? thought Aisha.

"That's not why I came over," Christopher protested. "Listen, the phone bill is due tomorrow."

"I know that," Kendra said. "How could I not know that? You left it on the pillow with all my calls highlighted."

"Are you ready to mail it in?" Christopher said.

Aisha sighed impatiently. Here she was given this perfect opportunity to eavesdrop without feeling guilty, and Christopher and Kendra couldn't come up with anything more interesting to talk about than the phone bill.

"Well, I'd better go," Christopher said.

"Good-bye, already," Kendra said.

"Listen, Kendra—"

"I know, I know, not a word to Aisha."

"If she finds out—" Christopher said grimly.

"She's not *going* to find out," Kendra said. "So please don't go into the big long list of all the dreadful things you'll do to me if she does."

Christopher said good-bye, and Aisha heard the door shut behind him. She heard Kendra's footsteps going back to the kitchen. She felt numb.

Steam was still rising from the bathwater, but a strange thing had happened. Aisha was covered with goose bumps.

Nine

Benjamin had always liked to walk in the rain, but this particular storm was a little forbidding, even for him. He was thinking about going home when he saw Nina walking toward him.

She was dressed like the Morton salt girl: slicker, boots, floppy hat. But unlike the Morton girl, who walked with a jolly, splashing gait, Nina walked with her head down, her feet shuffling.

"Nina," Benjamin called, but she didn't hear him.

She walked right up to him until her nose nearly bumped his chest and looked up in confusion. "Oh . . . hi," she said listlessly.

"You make a person feel warm all over," he said gently.

"I mean, hi, Benjamin!" she said obediently.

"That's better." He studied her face. Had she been crying? It was hard to tell in the rain. Raindrops had gathered on her eyelashes, forming sparkly crescents. Benjamin wanted to brush them away with his fingertips, but then he remembered: He didn't have the right to do that anymore.

He remembered talking to her in the back of the Sand Bar and saying, "I still love you."

And Nina saying, *"Still!"* with her voice full of tears.

He wished he could tell her that he hadn't meant it the way it sounded, but he wasn't sure he could explain exactly how he *had* meant it, so he didn't say anything.

Instead he fell in step beside her. "So, what are you doing out in this weather?"

"Hm? Oh, I needed to do some thinking," Nina said distractedly. She didn't ask him what he was doing out.

"How are things at home?"

"What? Oh, fine. Everyone's fine."

Benjamin realized that this was going to be a one-way conversation. "So . . . ," he said, casting about for something that might interest her. "Lara came over for lunch today."

"Everything go okay?"

"Yeah, amazingly," Benjamin said. He waited, but Nina said nothing more. Nina, who had once been so fascinated by the relationship between Lara and the Passmores. "What does she call your father?" she'd asked Benjamin a hundred times. "What does she call your *mother?* What did your father say when Lara said that? What do they talk about? Oh, you're so frustrating! You never remember anything!"

He studied her. What was she so preoccupied about?

She peered at him from under the brim of her hat. "What are you looking at?"

He smiled gently. "You. You have little droplets of water caught in the down on your upper lip, and they're catching the light."

"On my what?" Nina looked startled. "On my *mustache?"*

"No, I only meant—"

She smiled at his embarrassment. "I know what you meant," she said softly. "Thank you, I guess."

They were in front of his house. "Well, I think I'm going to go on in," Benjamin said awkwardly.

"Okay," Nina said. "I'm going to keep walking."

"More thinking to do?" he asked.

She shrugged.

"Bye."

"Bye."

Benjamin watched her walk away, stomping straight through every puddle. Nina had acted so differently toward him from yesterday. *What's changed?* he wondered.

The storm was letting up. It was just a summer shower and would pass them by, undamaged, after all.

Jake had been thinking about Kate so much that he could hardly believe his eyes when he saw her coming toward him, pulling a small red wagon full of dishes. But it really was her; he could see the newly emerged sun sparkling off her red hair.

She was deep in thought and didn't see him until she had walked right up to him.

"Hi," he said easily. "What are you doing?"

"I'm returning dishes to the neighbors for Mrs. Cabral," she said stiffly. She didn't look at him. When he didn't move out of her way, she pulled the wagon onto the grass.

"Kate," he said, catching her arm. "I want to explain about that letter—"

She jerked her arm out of his grasp. "You've had two days to work up an explanation," she said. "I'm sure it's a good one. I just don't want to hear it."

"It's not my fault you've refused to speak to me for two days," Jake said, exasperated. "I've called a million times. You don't return the calls."

Kate smiled painfully. "You're a slow learner, but you'll get it eventually," she said. "I don't want to talk to you."

Jake's mouth tightened angrily. *Fine,* he thought. *Have it your way.*

Kate tried to pull the wagon back onto the sidewalk, but the wheels had sunk down into the wet ground. He bent down automatically to help her.

"I'll do it," Kate snapped. She lifted the wagon back onto the sidewalk and slammed it down, unmindful of the clatter of dishes.

"Kate—" he said again.

But she was speeding away from him, the wagon whizzing behind her and her ponytail swaying angrily.

Jake stared after her, openmouthed. *Has she been taking her medication?* he wondered. Maybe . . . he didn't want to think this thought. *Maybe her mother is right.*

Nina

I loved Benjamin. I really did. I really _do._ Someday if they make a movie of my life, I want to make that perfectly clear, so they don't portray him as some youthful infatuation that I outgrew. (After all, he outgrew me, ha ha.)

It would be so much easier if we'd had one big huge major brawl. Then we could say we were sorry and make up. Or if we weren't sorry, at least I would have a nice, concrete reason for why we broke up. Something simple, so when people asked, I could say, "We broke up because (<u>fill in the blank</u>)." Instead all I can say is, "Um, we broke up because Benjamin developed new hobbies." And then I would have to list the five thousand things Benjamin decided he would rather do than spend time with me. And who wants an explanation that puts friends and acquaintances to sleep?

And now there's Lucas. Lucas, who was starting to like me—starting to pay attention to me. Naturally that had to get messed up, too. What's going to happen now?

Ten

"Hello?"

"Lucas, it's me."

"Hey."

"Can you talk?"

"Nina, you don't have to whisper."

"I guess . . . what are you doing?"

"Laundry. What are you doing?"

"Nothing."

"Oh. You want to do something tomorrow?"

"Do you think that's wise?"

"What do you mean?"

"Well, because of what happened today."

Silence.

"Lucas? Are you there?"

"I'm here. Nina, listen, I don't want to lose you over what happened today. We were both upset, it was a tense situation. It won't happen again."

"I don't want Zoey to get hurt."

"Neither do I. That's the most important thing, and we both agree on it. . . . So can we do something tomorrow?"

"Maybe the day after would be better."

"Okay. Just don't avoid me."

"I won't."

"Good."

"Lucas?"

"Yeah?"

"When you said you didn't want to lose me, did you mean you didn't want to lose my friendship?"

"Uh-huh. What did you think I meant?"

"Nothing, I guess. Good night."

"Good night."

"Hello?"

"Eesh?"

"Hi, Christopher . . ."

"What are you doing?"

"Just resting up for tomorrow. My mom has a big clean-a-thon planned."

"Sorry to hear it."

"How was work?"

"Brutal. Some woman sent her steak back three times."

"I heard once that you're never supposed to send stuff back because the cook spits on it."

"Well, I don't."

"I didn't mean you, personally. It was just something I heard."

"If I *were* ever going to spit on someone's steak, though, it would be this woman's. She sent it back twice because it was too rare, and then the third time she said it was too well-done."

"Too well-done? What were you supposed to do about it at that point?"

"Exactly."

"Hey, Christopher? Were you over at the house today?"

"Yeah, I wanted to talk to Kendra about the phone bill."

"Is everything okay between you and her?"

"As okay as it gets, I guess."

"Would you tell me if it weren't?"

"What do you mean?"

"I mean, would you tell me if you two were fighting about something specific?"

"Of course. I'm always honest with you, Eesh. It's the only way to be."

"Hello?"

"Mr. Norton?"

"Yes?"

"This is Claire Geiger."

"Oh, hi, Claire. How are you?"

"I'm fine, thanks. But I'd like to ask you a favor?"

"Sure thing. You want to borrow a cup of sugar or something?"

"No, I—I was wondering if, well, could you look out your window and tell me if you see anything unusual around our house?"

"Unusual?"

"Yes."

"I'm taking the portable phone to the window now. . . . Can you tell me what I'm looking for?"

"It's silly; I just thought I heard something."

"You think there's a prowler?"

"Oh, no, I'm sure I'm just being paranoid."

"What'd you hear?"

"Oh, it just sounded like someone trying one of the windows."

"Well, I don't see anything. You all alone over there, Claire?"

"I—yes. Everyone else went out to get a movie."

"You want to come over here and stay with us until they get back?"

"Oh, no, I—"

"Because I know what it's like when you think you hear something. You start looking at the windows and feeling nervous and then you start thinking, Who knows what might be out there looking *in*?"

"Gee, thanks, Mr. Norton. That cheered me right up."

"Sorry. Listen, how about if I got a flashlight and just took a quick look around?"

"Oh, you don't have to do that. I'm sure it was just a cat or something."

"You sound mighty shook up over just a cat."

"I . . ."

"I'll be right over."

"You're the greatest, Mr. Norton."

"Hello?"

"Lucas? You weren't asleep, were you?"

"Zoey! No, I'm awake."

"Well—I have great news!"

"Oh, tell me."

"I'm coming home!"

Silence.

"Lucas? Are you there?"

"Sure. I—I'm just surprised. Why are you coming back? What about your internship?"

"I'm miserable here. I hate my internship, I hate my roommate, I hate the weather. But mostly I miss you, Lucas. I don't want to spend any more of the summer away from you."

"Oh, babe . . . I know. When are you flying in?"

"I'm not flying. I'm taking the train. I'm actually calling you from the train station right now. They're having to route me through some crazy circuit. I think a covered wagon could get there faster than I'm going to."

"That doesn't matter. Just get here."

"You're happy I'm coming?"

"Of course I am."

"You sounded so strange there for a minute."

"I told you, I was just surprised. I love you, Zoey. I want to see you more than anything."

"Oh, Lucas, I love you, too."

"Hurry home, then."

"I am!"

"Zoey?"

"Hmmm?"

"I don't think I've ever loved you as much as I do right now."

"Oh, wow. What a wonderful thing to say. What a wonderful thing to hear. Oh, shoot, I've got to go."

"Don't miss the train."

"I *won't*. I love you. Bye."

"Bye."

Lucas hung up. He had meant every word.

Sweat streamed freely down Aaron's sides as he pushed the amplifier up Lighthouse Road. His guitar was balanced on the top. The damn thing must weigh a ton, no exaggeration. Plus a water taxi here, and for all he knew, another one back to Weymouth if Claire didn't invite him to stay. Of course, he could stay at the house without her permission. It was his house, too. But he wanted to wait until Claire asked him to stay.

The muscles in his arms were standing out like cords by the time he finally had urged the amp up the Geiger driveway. The house was in darkness. He paused, breathing heavily, his hands on his knees.

He straightened and unwound the amp's extension cord. Using a flashlight, he plugged it into the outside outlet that Burke normally used when barbecuing. He connected a few wires and was all set.

Aaron took off his T-shirt and mopped his face. He put the T-shirt back on and picked up his guitar. He settled the strap around his neck and took a deep breath. He played a few chords, the amp blaring. He was gratified to see windows light up all over the Geigers' house, as well as some of the neighbors'.

"Aaron?" his mother said sleepily from her and Burke's bedroom window. "Is that you? Is something wrong?"

"Nothing's wrong," Aaron said. "I'm just serenading Claire."

"Oh, Lord," he heard someone say faintly. He glanced up at the widow's walk. Claire was there, wearing a white nightgown that glowed in the moonlight. Her hair was a dark cloud against it.

"Well, go ahead, I guess," his mother said apprehensively. "But I thought you'd agreed to see other people—"

Aaron cut her off by playing a few more chords, deliberately making them harsh and discordant. He knew that most people, even his mother, thought he was a hack musician. He let the last chord spin out into the night, and then Aaron played the piece he had spent the afternoon learning. It was from *Romeo and Juliet*. A lovely piece, and Aaron made it even lovelier. The notes floated from his guitar in graceful smoothness, making everyone who heard it think of light-footed dancers. Aaron made the music coil in gentle, delicate spirals through the summer air. It puffed softly at the curtains of every window, and the last note hung on the air with an unbearable sweetness, like a nostalgia you feel as something is happening, before it is past.

"Oh, Aaron, that was so nice," his mother said softly.

"Not very original, though," Burke said.

"Dad!" It was Nina's voice. "Don't be an ogre. Don't you have any romance, any passion, in your soul?"

"No, I have an eight o'clock board meeting."

"Well, I thought it was the most beautiful thing I ever heard," Nina said. Her voice was melting with awe. Aaron wished Claire would say something so he could see if her voice sounded anywhere close.

But Claire was keeping her own counsel up there on the third floor, her elbows resting on the railing.

"Good night, Aaron," Burke said pointedly.

"Good night, honey," his mother echoed.

"Aaron?" Nina said.

"Yeah?"

"That was great."

"Thanks."

Nina shut her bedroom window.

"That was nice." Claire's voice floated down to him, noncommittal.

"Nice enough to invite me in?" Aaron asked.

"No."

"Oh."

"You can stay and talk to me for a while, though."

"From here?"

"Sure."

Aaron considered. He was surprised how easily he could hear her. "Okay." He sat down on the grass. "What should we talk about?"

"Books, movies, first-date stuff," Claire said. He

could hear a faint smile in her voice. "How many brothers and sisters we have."

He laughed. He supposed there was a chance that Nina and Burke and Sarah could hear their voices through their windows, but he didn't care. For once Aaron had nothing to hide.

Aisha

You know what's it's like when you walk into a room and everyone stops talking? You know what that feels like? How your face turns red and you stammer and drop things and pretend that you have some specific purpose, that you weren't just coming in to talk to a bunch of people who are obviously talking about _you?_

Well, that's how I feel all the time now. I feel like Christopher is always in the next room, talking about me. But it's like a maze, and no matter how fast I run, Christopher is always in just the next room.

Eleven

Aisha was in a bad mood, to put it mildly.

She stood in the attic with sweat gluing her T-shirt to her ribs and moisture collecting in the hollows of her collarbones. Her hair lay against her head like matted straw. Why had her mother decided the attic needed to be cleaned out in June, when it was five hundred degrees?

Because in a few months she won't have this free labor around, Aisha thought angrily, and irrationally, since her mother was paying her.

And stupid Kendra was supposed to be helping her, but Aisha's mother had sent Kendra off to get a guest's dry cleaning. Aisha thought grimly that Kendra would probably stretch that one five-minute errand into an hour at least. Aisha checked her watch. Kendra had already been gone for forty minutes.

Aisha looked around the attic in despair. It was so dusty and mildewy and cluttered. Plus you had to be careful where you stepped because only half of the attic floor was boarded. The other half was just fluffy pink insulation, and if you weren't careful, you could fall straight through into one of the guest rooms and break your leg.

That'll probably happen next, Aisha thought.

She already had a million bruises and a big lump on her head where she'd bumped a rafter. A shallow bright red scratch ran up the entire length of her right leg, the result of Aisha trying to move a mahogany dresser by herself. She thought ruefully that the scratch wasn't deep enough to require stitches. At least then she could have spent some relaxing time in the hospital.

She sighed. She might as well get moving; the attic wasn't going to clean itself, and Aisha wanted to be free this evening to see Christopher.

At the thought of Christopher, though, her eyes narrowed, and she felt even more annoyed. What was his secret? All his talk about honesty. What a damn hypocrite! Maybe she wouldn't see him tonight. Maybe she would just be by herself and do some lovely cool activity, like swim.

Aisha sighed again and picked up some crummy pottery vase that Kalif had made in camp once. *Why the hell is this even in the attic?* she wondered—and that's when the spider crawled out of the vase and bit her hand.

Aisha cried out and dropped the vase. She brushed at her hands frantically, but the spider had already fallen away. She examined her hand: a red swollen lump with a black dot in the center. She knew it was either going to itch or sting, probably both. She looked down angrily at the vase, which hadn't broken.

"*Damn* it!" Aisha said furiously.

She picked up the vase and threw it across the room as hard as she could. Again, it didn't break, which made her even angrier. She looked around hastily for something that *would* break, something that would satisfy her, that would fly into a trillion pieces. She grabbed an old chipped pitcher and held it over her head in both arms.

"What's going on?" Kendra inquired mildly. Aisha whirled around. She hadn't even heard her come up.

Kendra looked startled by the rage in Aisha's face. "What—what is it?" she asked warily.

Aisha took a step toward her. She had no idea what she was going to say until she said it. "I want you to tell me exactly what secret Christopher is keeping from me."

Kendra looked from Aisha's stony face to the upraised pitcher. She glanced behind her, but she was standing on the edge of the finished floor; behind her was nothing but insulation.

"What secret?" she asked, with not very convincing surprise.

"You know."

"He'll kill me if I tell you!" Kendra blurted.

Aisha was so surprised, she almost dropped the pitcher. After all this suspense someone had finally admitted that there *was* a secret. She took another step toward Kendra. Kendra backed away nervously.

"Kendra, you can't turn back now. I know so much already." Aisha lowered the pitcher but didn't put it down. She tried to make her voice gentle, coaxing. "I'm almost sure I know." She had no idea. "You can tell Christopher that I guessed and you just confirmed it."

Kendra stared at her with big eyes. She swallowed. "I wasn't exaggerating when I said he'd kill me."

Aisha advanced another step. Kendra stepped

98

back involuntarily and teetered on the edge of the flooring, the heels of her tennis shoes touching the insulation.

Aisha's hand flashed out automatically and caught Kendra's arm. Her only intention was pulling Kendra back, but Kendra obviously thought that Aisha might just as easily push her. She let out a little scream.

"Okay, okay," she said rapidly. "I'll tell you. Christopher was married before." She lifted her chin. "There. Now you know."

Zoey groaned and sat up as the train pulled into yet another station. She had been trying to sleep hunched over sideways in a double seat, but it was no good. Even when she did manage to fall asleep, the train would make another stop and wake her up.

She had told Lucas that it would be quicker to get to Maine by covered wagon. Well, that was an exaggeration, but it probably *would* actually be quicker by bicycle. Zoey ran a hand through her hair. It felt like waxed paper, greasy and stiff. Lord knew what she would look like when she finally saw Lucas.

Lucas. Zoey leaned back in her seat. He'd sounded odd on the phone, very odd.

Well, that's only to be expected, she told herself. *His father just died. Give him a break, why don't you.*

But Lucas hadn't sounded sad. Or even upset or depressed. He had sounded . . . distracted.

Zoey frowned. She knew she was being paranoid. She and Lucas had been through so much. They both had learned that secrets brought them nothing but trouble. She shouldn't let her mind work overtime. She should trust him—she *did* trust him. She trusted him with her life. She trusted him with her love.

A conductor was walking through the car.

"Excuse me," Zoey said, "but how long is this stopover?"

"Hour and a half," he said without pausing.

Zoey took her ticket and backpack and left the train station. She went directly to the telegraph office and sent a telegram to Lucas, telling him that she loved him.

Twelve

The library in Weymouth was all but empty, and Claire felt self-conscious as she crossed the main floor, the heels of her sandals clacking loudly. She supposed it wasn't surprising that the library was deserted. It was a beautiful summer day, and probably other people had better things to do.

But other people aren't being stalked, Claire thought. *Other people have all kinds of freedom. They don't know how lucky they are.*

She was wearing a flowered chiffon skirt and plain white blouse. Her dark hair was gathered at the nape of her neck and held there with a ribbon. She wore no makeup and a pair of Malcolm-X-type eyeglasses (no prescription) that she thought made her look studious.

She smiled automatically at the librarian behind the reference desk and sat at one of the library computer terminals.

The computer screen hummed blankly in front of her. Claire pressed the periodicals search key and waited for the prompt. Then she typed *stalkers* and pressed enter.

The computer hummed briefly and then displayed a list of ten thousand articles. The first piece was titled: "Stalkers: Case Studies in Terror."

No, thank you, Claire thought, pressing the search key again. *I have enough material for nightmares already.*

She typed *antistalking law* and pressed enter. This time the list was much shorter, and the articles seemed to be more what she wanted. Claire printed out the list and took it over to the reference librarian.

"Where can I find these?"

The librarian glanced at the list. "The periodicals section is in the basement. There's no one on duty to help you with microfiche, but the most recent twelve months of each subscription are on the shelves."

"That's fine," Claire said.

She went down two flights of stairs to the periodicals room. She took her list and began tracking down the first half dozen articles. She carried the magazines over to a carrel in the corner and began reading.

> *At first Marie Thompson, 25, thought the calls and letters were just random. "I thought it was like one of those chain letters you get out of nowhere," she says. "But then things began to get personal, very personal."*

Claire was relieved to see that Marie was still alive and well enough to be giving quotes. She skimmed ahead.

> *Stalking, commonly defined as "the willful, malicious, and repeated following or harassment of another person," is becoming more widespread in the United States. Victims of stalking are defined as those in danger of*

*physical and/or emotional harm. Women are
the victims of stalking far more often than
men. Stalking victims live with a daily measure
of fear that is unimaginable to most people.
Often they are forced to alter their lives per-
manently in order to find safety and freedom
from stalking by former spouses, ex-partners,
or strangers. Stalking can escalate to violence—and often does.*

Claire felt a strange sensation, and it took her a
second to pinpoint what it was. All the hairs on the
back of her neck were standing up. *Someone's
watching me,* she thought. *No, that's ridiculous; it's
just this stupid article. It's making my imagination
play tricks on me.*
She picked up the magazine again.

*Until 1990 restraining orders were the only
option available to stalking victims. Restraining orders are rarely effective because they
can only be put into effect after violence has
occurred—needless to say, they are sometimes
put into effect tragically after the fact. Police
could also use harassment or terrorist laws,
but harassment is only a misdemeanor offense.
Now all fifty states have some form of antistalking law. Police still require proof that the
stalker has "the ability to carry out their
threats," and often the burden is on the victim
to prove that the contact is "unconsensual" or
"undesirable."*

The feeling wasn't going away. Claire could
barely concentrate, the sensation of someone staring

at her was so intense. She turned around suddenly in her chair, surveying the room, but it was empty.

She shook her head. It was silly to try to read this creepy article alone in a dim, deserted room. She would only succeed in freaking herself out.

She shut the magazine. She would get a few others and then take them upstairs and have the reference librarian photocopy them. Then she could take them home and study them in her own nice, safe kitchen.

Claire picked up her list again and went back into the stacks. "Let's see," she said under her breath. "First *Newsweek.*" But she didn't like the sound of her slight whisper in the dry stacks, so she didn't say anything else. She found the *Newsweek*s and selected the right issue. She moved on toward the *U.S. News & World Report* section. Her heels were making an awful racket. She paused to take them off, and that's when she heard it.

Squeak.

The light touch of rubber soles on marble. Someone was in the basement with her. Someone wearing sneakers, in order to walk silently. In order to glide up behind her—

She whirled around.

The aisle was empty. But what about the aisle on either side of her? Claire's heart was beating too fast. She slipped her sandals off quickly and began tiptoeing back toward the stairs.

She took two light, quick steps and stopped.

Squeak.

It was coming from the aisle on her left. She waited, knowing that whoever was there was waiting for her to take another step. He would move with her, she was sure of that.

She took another step.

Squeak.

Perspiration made the black-rimmed glasses slippery on her nose. If she screamed, would the librarian be able to hear? Would she do anything? Would she do anything *in time?*

She took another step.

Squeak.

She took two steps.

Nothing.

Another.

Nothing.

Relief flooded through her. Probably she had been hearing nothing more than her own moist foot sticking to the floor—

Squeak.

Claire's control broke, and she bolted. She raced down the aisle, the harsh sound of her own panting loud in her ears. She reached the end of the aisle and realized too late that the stairs were out of reach. She would have to cross in front of the aisle on her left to get to them, and she *knew* suddenly that she didn't have enough of a head start. She knew that—

The aisle was empty.

Claire stopped the scream bubbling up inside her just in time. She stared at the empty aisle.

There was no shadowy figure, no madman in a ski mask, no one with a knife. No one at all. Claire almost couldn't believe it. She had been so *sure.* She had heard the squeaks, the unmistakable squeaks of tennis shoes. She hadn't just imagined it. She wasn't that paranoid.

. . . Stalking victims live with a daily measure of fear that is unimaginable to most people. . . .

She realized that she was still straining her ears

for the sound of footsteps. She took one more look at the empty aisle and then grabbed her purse from the carrel.

She didn't like turning her back on the room, and she flew up the stairs, three at a time. She burst onto the main floor like a diver breaking the water's surface and stood there, feeling faint.

Had she thought the main floor was deserted? Compared to the basement, it was booming with business. An old man was reading at a table, and a young woman was holding a little girl's hand over in the story corner. The reference librarian was still sitting serenely at her desk. The whole scene looked incredibly appealing to Claire: incredibly warm and happy and safe.

She walked carefully to a table near the old man. She would sit down and compose herself before going home. She realized that she left the magazines in the basement. Well, that was too bad; she wasn't going back into the basement for love nor money. Not with her imagination in overdrive like it was. She had been down there alone and nearly scared herself to death.

She reached into her purse for a Kleenex and paused. She frowned. Her purse was unzipped.

I never leave it unzipped, she thought, puzzled.

Another part of her mind was quicker to analyze the situation. *Don't reach in there,* it said. *You don't want to see it, whatever it is.*

But Claire's hand seemed to act of its own accord. It reached into her purse and pulled out a folded sheet of paper. Claire recognized it at once.

It was the page she'd torn out of Nina's true-crime book, the one with the photograph of the smiling, friendly-looking victim. Only now Claire's own face was on the victim's body.

                    *   *   *

Aisha had to sit down—her legs wouldn't support her. She sank down awkwardly onto the dirty attic floor, cradling the pitcher absently in her lap.

"Married?" she said wonderingly. But it wasn't really a question. Aisha knew from Kendra's voice that she was telling the truth. And it explained so many things: the tuxedo picture, the stories that didn't quite add up, Christopher's nervousness, the knowing looks, the whispered conversations, all of it. "When?" Aisha asked, still in the same stunned voice. "When was he married?"

Kendra sat down, too. "His junior year of high school."

"So young," Aisha said softly. "Why?"

Kendra shrugged. "Who knows with Christopher? He never tells anybody anything."

That's putting it mildly, Aisha thought.

"My mom accused him of wanting to rescue Carina," Kendra continued. "Carina didn't have a very good situation at home, from what I could tell. My mom said that it wasn't enough for Christopher just to date someone like everyone else; he had to charge in and take over her whole life, like Superman."

Aisha sighed. She could imagine Christopher doing that only too well. "Your mom didn't approve, I guess."

"She went through the roof," Kendra said. "She yelled at him for hours, saying he was throwing his life away, that he was still just a kid, what were they going to do for money, where were they going to live, that you can't just live on love alo—" She broke off hastily, as though realizing that maybe Aisha wouldn't want to hear about Christopher and this other girl's love.

"What did Christopher say?" Aisha asked.

Kendra smiled briefly. "Well, you know Christopher."

"Yes." *At least I thought I did,* Aisha added silently.

"He said that he would handle everything. That he would drop out of school and get a job. That Carina—"

"Carina what?"

"Carina Connelly."

It was a pretty name. "What did she look like?" Aisha asked. Then she cringed. *Am I that shallow?* she thought. *That I have to ask what she* looked *like?*

But Kendra didn't seem to find the question odd. She looked thoughtful. "She was very—delicate. She was short and had great big eyes and lots of curly hair. It hung all the way down her back. She used to wash it at night, and it would take hours to dry. She and Christopher lived with us for a month; that's how I know."

"And then they got their own apartment?" Aisha asked.

Kendra nodded. "But three weeks later he moved back home."

"Just him?" Aisha asked. "Not her?"

Kendra nodded again.

"Three *weeks?*" A month living with his mother and three more weeks on their own. *Seven weeks,* Aisha thought. *So short.*

"Why—" She stopped. She had been about to ask Kendra when Christopher had last seen Carina, but why ask Kendra? Why not go directly to the source?

She stood up.

"Where are you going?" Kendra asked nervously.

"To Passmores'," Aisha said. "To see Christopher."

Kendra looked uncomfortable. "Could you, uh, maybe not tell him I told you?"

"Do you think he won't figure it out?" Aisha asked. "Besides, there have been way too many lies already."

Kendra sighed, looking resigned. "He's not at Passmores'," she said wearily. "He went to the dentist."

"Which one?"

"Which one what?"

"Which dentist?"

Kendra looked puzzled. "Dr. Derry in Weymouth," she said. "Why? You're not going to go there, are you?"

"Watch me," said Aisha.

She walked down the attic stairs and then down another flight onto the main floor and out the back door. There was an outdoor shower by the back door, Mrs. Gray's attempt to keep guests from tracking sand all over the place.

Aisha pulled the string and stuck her head under it. She didn't even feel the icy downpour. The water lasted for thirty seconds, but Aisha was already walking away before it stopped.

She began marching toward the ferry, squeezing the water from her hair. The combination of June weather and her steaming anger dried it in no time.

Thirteen

Lara set up her easel in the kitchen. She was planning to do her first preliminary sketch of Mr. Passmore sitting at the kitchen table. Mr. Passmore was upstairs, changing.

Benjamin was perched on one of the stools at the breakfast bar, watching her. "You know, my dad is so excited about this, he can barely stand it," he said.

Benjamin thought it was pretty exciting just to look at Lara. He thought she always looked great, but today she looked more than great; she looked magnificent. She was wearing faded old jeans that rested low on her hips and a ratty old T-shirt. The T-shirt didn't quite reach the top of her jeans, and whenever she raised her arm, Benjamin could see the curve of her stomach. She wore no makeup, and her platinum hair was rumpled. She reminded Benjamin of Nina.

"It's not such a big deal," Lara said.

"I think it's a big deal," Benjamin said. He didn't push the point, though, because although he truly did think it was great, he knew that if you say that too much, it sometimes sounds like you really mean the opposite. Instead he said, "Let me wipe the table; otherwise you'll have to immortalize that big smear of alfredo sauce." He stood up to get the sponge.

"I love alfredo sauce," Lara said, adjusting her easel.

"Well, you might love *good* alfredo sauce," Benjamin said. "But I don't think you'd have loved mine. It makes a pretty strong adhesive," he added, scrubbing at the spot. "Dad is going to teach me how to make it, though. We've agreed to set up meetings at the restaurant—like a cooking class; he'll teach me everything he knows about pasta."

"A cooking class?" Lara asked.

He nodded.

"Just for pasta dishes?" Lara said. "How cool."

"Why don't you come, too?" Benjamin said.

She looked surprised. "You and me? And—our dad?"

"Sure," Benjamin said. "Why not?"

"Well—how many classes?"

"Six," Benjamin said. "Every Monday and Wednesday for three weeks."

"Three weeks," Lara repeated softly, as though to herself.

Benjamin smiled at her indecision. "I realize it's a big, huge commitment," he teased. "But I think our friendship can withstand it."

Lara met his eyes, and suddenly she smiled. It lit up her face. "I'd love to," she said.

"I'll call you," Benjamin said.

Mr. Passmore came into the kitchen. "Sorry to keep you waiting," he said, sitting at the table. "But I changed shirts about ten times. What do you want me to do?"

"Just sit there naturally," Lara said. She picked up

111

her charcoal and studied Mr. Passmore. "You don't look very natural," she said.

"It's hard," Mr. Passmore said. "I'm too excited."

"But you look like—like a stuffed deer," Lara protested. "You have exactly the same expression as a doe mounted over a fireplace. All alert and eager to please."

"I *am* alert and eager to please," Mr. Passmore said, puzzled.

"Yes, and it's showing in every line of your face," Lara said. "Benjamin, fix him a snack. Maybe it'll help him relax."

Benjamin had actually been thinking about going upstairs and lying down. He had a headache. But he climbed off the stool obediently and said, "What would you like, Dad?"

"Some graham crackers and a glass of grape juice," Mr. Passmore said.

"Coming right up." Benjamin bent to get the box of graham crackers out of the cupboard.

"How old are you?" Lara asked.

"Forty-four," Mr. Passmore said. "Why?"

"Because that's the kind of snack a kindergartner would ask for," Lara said.

Benjamin hid a smile as he shook a few crackers onto a plate. He poured a glass of juice and carried both the juice and the plate to the table.

"Thanks," Mr. Passmore said. "So, listen, can you airbrush out my wrinkles?"

"For both our sakes, I'm going to consider that a joke," Lara said. "Ha ha."

Mr. Passmore laughed, and to Benjamin's surprise, Lara did, too.

"Now, hush and eat your snack," Lara ordered, but she was smiling.

Benjamin leaned against the refrigerator. His headache was picking up steam. In a minute he would take some aspirin and drink a Coke.

The phone rang.

"I'll get it," Mr. Passmore said with his mouth full. "It might be Zoey." He shoved back his chair and sped into the living room.

Lara threw her piece of charcoal on the table so hard that a corner crumbled. She walked across the kitchen and began washing her hands.

"Hi, honey," Mr. Passmore said in the living room.

"This is ridiculous," Lara said, glancing at the clock. "We're not going to get anywhere at this rate."

Benjamin wondered where her good mood of a minute ago had gone.

"This is *ridiculous,*" Lara said again, half to herself.

What happened next was totally involuntary. Benjamin's hand darted out and clasped Lara's elbow. He closed his eyes and let his other senses do the work, the way he had when he was blind.

He felt Lara's tension. He felt her hostility surging past him into the living room. What was in the living room? His father—his father, talking to Zoey. At the same time Benjamin smelled the red wine bottle in the wastebasket. It was empty; only a few drops clung to the green glass bottom. But those drops smelled so good, so delicious, so thirst quenching. Benjamin knew that he was smelling what Lara smelled, what Lara wanted.

It all happened in a matter of seconds.

Lara jerked her elbow away. "What did you do that for?" she asked irritably.

It was a good question. Why had he done something a blind person would do, when he could *see?*

Dr. Derry smiled reassuringly at Christopher. She tapped the nitrous oxide mask over his nose. "Are you relaxed yet?"

He nodded.

"Not nervous, are you?" Dr. Derry said gently. "It's just one cavity."

"I'm okay," Christopher said thickly.

"Good." Dr. Derry reclined the chair. "Now just breathe deeply and relax. You're going to hear a drill, but the sound is worse than it feels."

Christopher inhaled, not minding the sickly sweet smell of nitrous oxide. The room was air-conditioned, with boring elevator music piped in. Dr. Derry dabbed something minty flavored on his gum. Christopher stared at the poster on the ceiling. It was of a kitten tied up in a ball of yarn, and the caption said: Hang in there, baby. Christopher wondered why Dr. Derry didn't put up a more interesting poster—she certainly charged enough—and then his eyelids closed.

The drill began its high-pitched whine, and he felt pressure against his tooth.

"There," Dr. Derry said in her soft, hypnotic way. Christopher opened his eyes briefly. She was holding a small strip of metal with a pair of tweezers. "I'll just fit this in and then size it, and you'll be through."

He closed his eyes again. He heard the scrape as the strip of metal was fitted between his molars, and then the buzz of the drill resumed. It stopped abruptly.

"You *bastard,*" a voice hissed in his ear. The

voice was so filled with rage, he barely recognized it.

Christopher's eyes flew open. "Aisha?"

She was standing over his chair, her cheeks flushed, her clothes covered with streaks of dirt, her hair a mass of tiny waves and curls.

"Miss, this is a private treatment room," Dr. Derry said. "You're going to have to leave."

Aisha ignored her.

Christopher took one look at her and thought: *She knows.*

Aisha seemed to read the look in his eyes. "Yes," she said grimly. "I know. So sit up and start talking."

Christopher couldn't have talked if he want to because Dr. Derry still had the drill in his mouth. He gestured futilely.

"Miss, I really must insist that you leave," Dr. Derry said.

Aisha didn't take her eyes off him. "Christopher and I need five minutes alone," she said. "And then you can pull every one of his teeth, for all I care."

Dr. Derry looked a little taken aback. "He's in the middle of a procedure."

Christopher tried to spit out the drill, but his tongue was too numb.

"It's important," Aisha said. She was clearly not going anywhere.

Dr. Derry studied her. "Okay," she said at last. She pulled the drill out of Christopher's mouth like someone putting a car in park. "Five minutes," she said, closing the door behind her.

Christopher tried to sit up, but Dr. Derry had reclined the chair so far that his head was practically pointing at the floor. All he could do was crane his neck up. "What did Kendra—"

"Never *mind* what Kendra told me!" Aisha shouted. "I want to hear it from you. Go ahead, tell me all about how you didn't tell me for my own good, or how the past is the past, or how you were going to tell me soon. Go on! I can't wait."

Christopher was suddenly aware of the tray of dental instruments next to him. What if Aisha stabbed him with a scalpel or a drill or something?

"I'm waiting, liar," Aisha said.

Christopher was trying to think, trying to clear his head of the nitrous oxide fog. "I—I never lied to you," he said weakly.

"Don't you split hairs with me," Aisha said. "You now have three and a half minutes, and then I walk out of here."

"Can't we—can't we discuss this later? I need—"

"Why? So you can have time to get your story straight?" Her eyes were full of tears, but her voice was hard. "Start talking and make it the truth, or I'm leaving."

Christopher rubbed his temples. "Okay," he said, his mind racing. "I was married when I was sixteen. It lasted about five minutes."

"It lasted seven weeks!"

"Aisha—" He reached for her hand, but she jerked it away from him. "Eesh, it was over before it started. We had it annulled—"

"Oh, and that means it doesn't count?" She crossed her arms. "If this marriage was so *insignificant,*" she said, her voice dripping with sarcasm, "why didn't you bother to tell me?"

Christopher felt his own anger building, irrational or not. "Listen, what happened with Carina is history, okay?"

"When you love someone, you love their history,

too!" Aisha spat out. "When you marry someone, you want everything—future, present, past."

"Carina had a certain set of problems," Christopher said. "I don't want to discuss it."

"You don't want to discuss it!" Aisha shrieked. "Well, you'd better start wanting to discuss it, or it's over between us, Christopher."

"Don't give me ultimatums," Christopher said, his voice deadly. "We don't need to discuss it. Carina has nothing to do with you."

A silence more awful than Aisha's shouting filled the room.

"I see," Aisha said. "Is that your final word?"

"Yes."

"Well, then, this is mine. From now on *you* have nothing to do with me, either."

She turned and left him sitting there, still wearing the blue paper dental bib and tasting amalgam, which tasted just like copper pennies, or fear.

Zoey

At first the train was exciting because I kept thinking that someone was going to get murdered. Then I realized that I was only thinking about that movie, Murder on the Orient Express. In reality it's pretty monotonous.

All I do is try to sleep, write in my diary, and read my book, and every few hours I wander up to the service car and buy something fattening to eat. God knows what I'm go to weigh when I finally step off of here.

Oh, wait, there's one other thing I do: I think about Lucas. There's a lot to think

about. I can obsess
about how he must hate
me for leaving him just
after his father died. I
can fret about how little
time we have left together
before I leave. Did I
just say that this train
ride was monotonous?
What? With all this to
think about? Is this
what my dad meant by
"getting my head together"?
It feels more like having
it fall apart.

The other thing I like
to do is look out the
window at the passing
scenery. When I was lit-
tle and had to fly on an
airplane, I used to imag-
ine that the plane
wasn't really going any-
where—that people were
scurrying around outside
the plane changing the

set, like in a movie. And when I'd step off, I wouldn't have gone anywhere, but everything would look different. In a train you can feel the miles chugging by. The distance is very real.

I'm starting to worry about going to college next fall. The distance between Maine and California is huge. How will I be able to stand the thought of all those miles between me and Lucas?

Fourteen

Claire sat in the diner across from the library, toying with a grilled cheese sandwich and drinking a strawberry milk shake. She kept checking the shoes of everyone in the diner, to see who was wearing sneakers.

She was on her third milk shake. She kept ordering them because she was afraid to open her purse, afraid to leave the diner, afraid to get in her car and drive home. Afraid, period.

The page from Nina's true-crime book was spread out in front of her. Claire had been studying it for hours. She knew the photograph that had been pasted over the victim's face. It had appeared in the Weymouth paper last fall, with the dumb caption, Local Girl Cheers Team to Victory, which made Claire sound like a cheerleader, instead of just a girl watching a game.

Later, the newspaper photographer had told her that he was hoping to get a profile shot, but Claire had seen him out of the corner of her eye and turned. The picture was beautiful. Claire was looking directly into the camera, a small I-caught-you-looking-at-me smile playing at the corners of her lips, her dark hair spilling over her shoulders.

The grainy newspaper print was what had fooled Claire into thinking it was actually her face on the victim's body. Now she used the edge of her fingernail and scraped the newspaper picture off. The real victim's face was still beneath, stained by glue.

He went through our garbage to get this, Claire thought. *He pawed through God knows how many orange peels and coffee grinds and Kleenex and found it. And then he guessed. No, he* knew. *He* knew *that I had cut that page out of Nina's book and thrown it away because it frightened me. Oh, he must've been so happy, so satisfied, when he found it.*

She tried to remember when she'd thrown it out. It was only a few days ago, and garbage day was today. Janelle emptied all the wastebaskets on Sunday morning and put the cans out Sunday night.

What if I had looked out my window and seen a dark figure out by the curb? she thought in a sudden panic. *Maybe he was there the whole time Aaron was serenading me. Maybe there was someone waiting. . . .*

She knew it was possible; she could have seen him. She didn't want to do that, not ever. Scared as she was of the stalker, she was certain he would be even more frightening if she ever laid eyes on him. She always imagined him as a man with a ski mask on. She saw it over and over in her nightmares, a masked face bending over her while she tried desperately to recognize the eyes.

How close had he been to her this morning? He must've run the other way when she ran for the stairs; that was the only explanation for the empty aisle. But for a few moments at least they must've been next to each other, separated only by a shelf of magazines. What if she had reached blindly through the magazines and let her hand extend into the next aisle? Would he have held still while her fingers moved toward him? And he surely wasn't wearing a mask in the library. Would her fingers have touched his cheek, his hair? Would he have smiled when she reached for him?

The image was scaring Claire so badly, she tried not to think about it anymore. She stared instead at her purse. She didn't want to reach into it again. Who knew what she would find? And how could she look at her wallet, her compact, knowing that *he* had touched them?

On the other hand, it was getting late and Claire was tired of sitting in the diner. She wanted to go home, but first she would need to pay her bill and get her car keys.

She pinched the bottom seam of her purse and held it upside down. The contents tumbled onto the table: wallet, keys, compact, lipstick, packet of tissues, a ticket stub, directions to the Sand Bar, a container of dental floss. Claire wanted to laugh with relief. Just the usual junk, nothing sinister. She gathered up everything except her wallet and keys and threw it in the diner's wastebasket. She couldn't wear makeup that he had touched. The thought made her nauseous. Thank God her keys were here; otherwise she would never be able to feel safe again.

She paid the check, left a tip, and walked outside. The sun felt warm and comforting after the air-conditioned diner. She looked at the library. Now it seemed like just another neat, friendly brick building, not the set of a horror film.

She walked across the street to the library parking lot. It was only three-thirty; she had plenty of time to catch the four o'clock ferry. She decided to drive to The Body Shop and buy some bubble bath. A long bath tonight was what she needed, reading something very nonsuspenseful, like *Emma*.

She parked in front of the Body Shop and locked the car doors carefully. She went inside and spent a happy few minutes poring over the bubble bath selection. She finally settled on a vanilla one that smelled like cake batter, paid, and went back outside.

She knew something was wrong instantly. The lock button was raised on the driver's-side door. But Claire had locked it; she was sure she had. She glanced around. It was a busy parking lot; nothing could happen to her here, could it? Besides, Claire's instincts told her that the stalker wasn't nearby. She couldn't feel him that way she had in the library. He wasn't here. But he'd *been* here, she was positive.

On the ferry back she would just sit in the car the whole way, with the doors locked.

She approached the car slowly, after noticing that all the lock buttons were raised. She set her paper bag on the hood and looked inside cautiously. There was a slip of paper on the driver's seat. Everything else looked normal.

Claire looked around her again. There were plenty of people. She opened the car door and reached for the piece of paper. It was written in the same block printing as the messages on the backs of the photographs:

Claire, you should have looked in the backseat.

She didn't hesitate now. She dropped the note and wrenched open the back door, leaning inside, whispering to herself, "Oh, no, oh, no; please, don't let it be."

But it was just as she feared. The backseat was warm to her touch.

Aisha walked back to the ferry landing, her anger evaporating, a sort of numb confusion taking its place. The sun had slipped behind some clouds, and Aisha shivered.

The ferry was leaving; she had to run to catch it. A man near the gate reached out his hand and helped her jump aboard.

"Thanks," Aisha breathed.

"My pleasure," the man said. He took a seat and shook out a newspaper.

Aisha thought it was incredible that this man—that anyone—could touch her and not know instantly that something was wrong. Couldn't he feel the heartbreak coming off her in thick, heavy waves? She was honestly surprised that he hadn't stopped and taken both her hands, saying, "Miss, isn't there something I can do?"

Aisha realized she was still standing by the gate. She moved over to the railing so the breeze was full in her face.

Christopher was married.

Christopher's marriage was annulled.

Christopher never told her either of these facts.

His former wife's name was Carina.

Carina was petite.

Carina had big, beautiful eyes.

Carina had a cloud of long, dark hair.

Aisha found that she could hardly get any of these facts to penetrate her brain. She knew them all, but she didn't quite believe them; she didn't accept them as facts yet. And wasn't part of her hoping, way down deep, that it wasn't true? That Christopher could still somehow *(but he can't, he can't)* explain it all away?

Aisha reviewed her list of facts again and decided to concentrate on the last one. Carina had a cloud of long, dark hair. She used to wash it at night, and it would take hours to dry. Where did she sit while it dried? On Christopher's bed? Did he stand behind her, arranging the damp tendrils into corkscrews, smelling her shampoo, whatever it was: vanilla, orange blossoms, honeysuckle?

Suddenly Aisha thought of the girl she had seen Christopher with all those months ago, the girl in the Daisy Dukes, the girl with the blond hair so long she could sit on it—and a sob escaped her. She hadn't known she was so close to tears. She very nearly glanced around to see where the sound had come from.

But now there was no calling back the tears. They came freely, and Aisha buried her face in her hands and cried into the wind on the ferry. She cried over Carina and the other girl and her own perfectly lovely but merely shoulder-length hair. She cried over Christopher and his lies, his lies on top of other lies, and his refusal to give her what she really wanted: answers.

He had *lied* to her. Every time he had failed to tell her about Carina, every opportunity he had passed up in the year they'd known each other— every time he had decided not to tell her was as good as a lie. How would she ever, ever trust him again?

As her tears tapered off, Aisha noticed a woman and her daughter looking at her in a concerned way.

She shrugged self-consciously and tried to smile. They looked away.

Aisha wiped her eyes with the back of her hand and thought about how once when she was twelve, she had seen a man and a woman arguing in a restaurant, and the woman was crying. Aisha had assumed the man was breaking up with the woman. Now, looking back, she still thought that. But at the age of twelve she had imagined that the woman would cry and later splash a little water on her face, and by the next day she would be flirting with the dishwasher repairman and thinking that perhaps life was worth living after all.

Now Aisha knew better. Now she knew that there were wounds so serious that the end of the pain was nowhere in sight.

Fifteen

Claire opened her bedroom door and looked out into the hall. The light was off, and the switch was at the bottom of the stairs. She took a deep breath and began to descend quickly. She reached the bottom and curled her hand cautiously around the corner, feeling for the light switch—

Her fingers touched another hand.

Claire let out a small scream before light flooded the landing and she saw Nina standing there.

"What are you doing, lurking around in the dark?" Claire snapped.

"Excuse me," Nina said, "but I happen to live here, remember? I was just coming up the stairs; it's not my fault the light was out."

"Well, then, you should make more noise and not go *sneaking* around—"

"Claire? Why don't you call your old shrink and have her prescribe some Valium because you are really driving me crazy with all this paranoia."

"Paranoia?" Claire said through gritted teeth.

"Yes, paranoia," Nina said. "So we've gotten a few crank calls from some creep who saw your picture in the yearbook. That's no reason to be so highstrung. It's making you hard to live with."

"Hard to live with?" Claire flared. "What about you, wandering around and sighing all the time like some lovesick little—"

Nina's brows rushed together. "I am *not*—"

"You are, too! Tonight when Dad was playing that dumb Frank Sinatra album, you were all but singing along and your eyes were all glazed over. It was sickening."

"Shut up, Claire!"

But Claire continued venomously. "I don't think you're even upset about Benjamin, because he hates Frank Sinatra. So I'd really like to know just who—"

"*I'd* really like to know just who tore a page out of one of my true-crime books," Nina said heatedly. "Although I have a pretty good idea. Remember when you were little and you made Dad keep *Where the Wild Things Are* in his bedroom because you were too scared?"

From downstairs in the living room they heard Burke say to Sarah, "I offered to take them to the circus."

"God!" Nina shouted. "That's so irritating!"

"Just stay out of it, Dad!" shouted Claire.

Burke tried to whisper. "I know—"

"Shut up!" both girls shouted, finally in agreement about something.

Kalif stood in the doorway of Aisha's room, absently plopping the softball into his mitt. "Eesh, can we play catch when Christopher comes over?"

"No." Aisha was rearranging her bureau drawers with the restless energy of the heartbroken. She shook all her underwear onto the bed.

"Why not? Christopher said he was going to teach you not to throw like such a girl."

"Kalif, that is a horrible, sexist expression you picked up from Christopher, and I never want to hear you use it again."

"Oh." Kalif dropped the ball a few more times. "Is Christopher coming over tomorrow?"

"No," Aisha said, emptying her sock drawer onto the bed.

"Why not? Isn't he your boyfriend anymore?"

"Nope," she said grimly.

"Why—"

"Kalif, two-year-olds say *why* all the time. Do you think you could either come up with something better or leave me alone?"

Kalif thought for a minute. "How come he's not—"

"Oh, for God's sake," Aisha snapped. "Stop bothering me."

"Can I call Christopher and see if he wants to play catch?"

"Absolutely not."

"Why?"

"Because he's my boyfriend, and I don't want you—"

"You just said he wasn't your boyfriend anymore," Kalif corrected.

"Kalif," Aisha said slowly. "Get out of my sight. Right now. Right this instant."

"But why—"

She picked up an embroidered pillow and threw it. It hit the ground three yards in front of Kalif.

"See?" he said happily. "You do throw like a girl."

Lucas hammered on Kate's door. "Kate, your mom's on the phone."

She opened the door. "Tell her I'm not home."

Lucas looked annoyed. "I'm not your social secretary."

Kate looked equally irritated. "I'm not asking you to be. I'm just asking you to deliver a simple message."

"If it's so simple, why don't you deliver it yourself?"

"Because I don't feel like it."

"Well, maybe I don't feel like it, either."

"Look, Lucas, just do it, okay? I didn't feel like having that long talk with your aunt Ginger about how I have the hips of a natural childbearer, but I did it to be polite."

"So?" said Lucas. "Is that supposed to make me happy? I couldn't care less if you'd spit on my aunt Ginger."

"Well, then, hang up on my mother," Kate said. "That way it'll free up the line for you and Nina to have another whispered conversation."

"Leave Nina out of this," Lucas snapped.

"Then tell my mother I'm not home," Kate said. She shut her door.

Lucas thought about kicking it, but he knew he was the one who'd have to repair the scuff mark, so in the end he went downstairs and told Kate's mother that Kate wasn't home.

Kendra was eating from a bag of Cheetos when Christopher walked in. Her hand tightened reflexively and crushed the bag.

The left side of Christopher's jaw was swollen. "Oh, yes," he said slowly to Kendra, his voice shaking with fury. "That's right. You'd *better* look scared."

Kendra sank back against the chair cushions. "Christopher, I didn't have a choice."

"Tell me about it," Christopher said quietly. "I don't want you to think I didn't listen to your side of the story before I kill you."

"No, it's true!" Kendra protested. "She was threatening me with a pitcher—" Kendra looked up at him guiltily from her cloud of orange Cheetos dust. "Okay, if you're going to kill me," she tried to bluff, "then go ahead."

Christopher grabbed for her, and she screamed. She squirted out of his arms as though she were greased and jackrabbited across the apartment to her room.

Christopher swore, his hands clenching into fists. He picked up the chair Kendra had been sitting in and almost threw it out the window. He longed to break something, to see the window shatter into a thousand shimmering shards of glass.

He stood undecided for a moment and then let the chair drop so rapidly that it jammed his thumb.

Christopher held the injured thumb against his chest, tears oozing out from under his closed lids. He folded his tall body awkwardly onto the floor next to the chair and cried, rocking back and forth, his head bent.

He stayed that way all night, not even stopping when Kendra at last edged out of the bedroom and came close enough to stroke his hair.

Claire

I keep thinking about him going through the trash. I mean, obviously if he did it once, he's done it a bunch of times. So, really, the question is: What have I thrown away?

Okay, let's think. Old clothes. He can have them. Old makeup, ditto. Old letters? Well, I'm not thrilled about that. What else do people throw away? Kleenex, ferry tickets, homework papers, broken china, food containers, telephone messages, magazines, newspapers, dust balls, gum wrappers, string, rubber bands, keys.

Well, there's an interesting idea:

133

keys. House keys. But people don't throw them away. Do they? Do they? No. Of course, not. So there's still one place I'm perfectly safe.

Sixteen

Nina couldn't sleep. She had been trying for hours, staring at the ceiling, curling up on her side, closing her eyes and trying to count backward from one hundred. Now it was two in the morning and she was lying on her belly, her hand touching the floor and one foot kicking lazily at the mattress. She was miles from sleeping. She was about as far from sleeping as you could be.

Zoey was coming home tomorrow.

The thought filled Nina with dread, and then the thought that she could feel that way about her best friend filled her with *more* dread.

Because of their new unlisted phone number Zoey hadn't been able to call and tell Nina—Nina felt a deep rush of gratitude toward the crank caller; what would she have said to Zoey?—but Mr. Passmore had seen her on the street and told her that Zoey was coming home early. Nina had felt her blood go cold, all the while she smiled and nodded and said, yes, it was wonderful news, and of course she would be there for the homecoming dinner.

Nina was wearing a nightgown she had bought at a thrift shop. It was pale blue silk, with a high fitted bodice and odd petal-shaped sleeves. It would have been absolutely lovely if it didn't have a big bleached spot on the shoulder. Nina wondered if she would sleep better in a T-shirt, but she didn't get up and change.

Zoey is coming home, she thought for the millionth time. *Tomorrow. Zoey is going to come home. She's going to be in the same room with me. What am I going to do?*

If only Zoey had come home a couple of days ago! Then none of this would have happened. If Zoey had come home on Saturday, she would have been the one to comfort Lucas after his mother told him he couldn't go to college. And Zoey would also have been the one to comfort Nina after her breakup with Benjamin. Nina and Zoey could have walked on the beach together and comforted each other, just like Nina and Lucas had done, only without the kiss, of course.

And if the kiss had never happened, Nina would be looking forward to having Zoey home. Nina had missed Zoey. She had missed the long, lazy afternoons of talking about absolutely nothing for two or three hours and then trying to trace the various threads of their conversation back to the beginning. They never could. She had missed sunbathing in Zoey's backyard, missed calling Zoey after spending all day with her and still having so much to talk about that Nina's father would stand by the phone making scissor-cutting motions with his fingers. She missed—

Oh, yeah, I missed Zoey so much I kissed her boyfriend, Nina thought.

She sat up. She couldn't take another minute of lying in bed and thinking these same thoughts over and over. She wanted to go out for a walk.

She slipped down the stairs and out the front door, looking like a pale blue ghost of herself, off in search of someplace to haunt.

2:01.

Lucas stared at the kitchen clock, his eyes feeling as bright and red as the digital numbers. He stirred the saucepan of milk.

Lucas had no idea if warm milk actually did help you sleep or if that was just an old wives' tale. He only knew that he was desperate. He would try anything.

He had been trying to fall asleep since nine o'clock. That was—he counted briefly—five hours. What a waste of time. If he'd known he wasn't going to fall sleep, he could have gotten up and at least done something fun instead of lying in bed, worrying about Zoey coming home tomorrow.

The milk was steaming slightly, and Lucas poured it into a mug. He wished Zoey were coming home a few days from now so that he and Nina would have a chance to straighten things out. Just how they were going to go about that, he didn't know. He only knew that they had to, they *had* to. Lucas wasn't going to screw things up with Zoey again.

He wondered, not for the first time, why he kept making mistake after mistake in his relationship with Zoey. The relationship was what he loved and valued most in his life. He would have done *anything* for Zoey. So why did he keep screwing up?

Not that he had screwed up, he reminded himself hastily. Zoey didn't know about this kiss with Nina, and there was no reason she ever had to find out. And even if she did find out, Lucas was sure that Zoey would understand—

Maybe

—because she loved both Lucas and Nina and she would know that they were only turning to each other out of loneliness, that it meant nothing, that . . .

The milk tasted awful. Lucas poured it down the sink and went for a walk.

Because North Harbor was such a small town, Nina wasn't at all nervous about going for a midnight walk by herself in a nightgown. And also because it was such a small town, there were a limited number of places to go. Nina walked toward the town center. She wasn't going to Lucas's house, she decided. She wasn't even going to walk by and see if his bedroom light was on . . .

. . . Lucas walked along South Street. Zoey was coming home. There was nothing he could do about that, and he wouldn't have done anything even if he could have. He was happy she was coming home. But how long was she going to be here? A few weeks? Then she'd be off to California, and what was he supposed to do then? Absently Lucas turned right on Camden Street . . .

. . . Nina's feet seemed to have a mind of their own. They were leading her to Zoey's house, and she definitely didn't want to go there. She would have to go there tomorrow, though, for Zoey's homecoming dinner. If anyone else's parents planned something like that, it wouldn't work. The guests would resent it, and the guest of honor would be tired and irritable and think it was dumb. Not with Zoey, though. She would walk in and be funny and gracious and beautiful and herself, and Lucas's heart would melt, right along with everyone else's . . .

. . . It was just a kiss, Lucas told himself angrily. He and Nina would work past it. He would keep this one last secret from Zoey and wipe the slate clean. He and Nina would repair their friendship. All three of them would be happy. Lucas would see to it . . .

. . . As she crossed the town center Nina tortured herself with a fantasy of what would happen if Zoey found out. Would there be tears and recriminations? Zoey had been furious when Lucas made out with Claire, but how would she feel about Nina? Well, she wouldn't be *happy;* Nina couldn't fool herself that much. But she wouldn't be threatened, either, because it was Nina we were talking about here. Not some raving beauty . . .

Lucas looked up suddenly. Exchange Street. He was going toward Nina's house. Well, what harm was there in that? She would be asleep. But even if she wasn't, even if her bedroom light was on, he wasn't going to do anything. He wasn't going to throw a pebble at her window. He wasn't . . . Lucas turned a corner and bumped right into Nina, who was wearing some crazy, ugly, wonderful nightgown and looking so sexy that he wondered, actually *wondered,* if he were home in bed and dreaming.

"Lucas!" Nina said, startled. She was obviously not a dream. "What are you doing here?"

He shrugged. "I couldn't sleep."

"Same here," Nina said. "My mind was racing. I kept thinking about, you know—things."

Yes, I know about—things, Lucas thought.

They fell into step beside each other. Lucas was suddenly aware that he was only wearing a baggy pair of sweats. He wondered why he felt self-conscious about that when Nina didn't seem to care that she was only wearing a filmy nightgown.

"So are you going to Zoey's homecoming?" Nina asked him.

"Sure," Lucas said. "Are you?"

She nodded, and he thought, *She has to go. She's the Best Friend. Just like I'm the Boyfriend.*

"Did Mr. Passmore tell you it was a potluck?" Nina said. "What are you going to bring?"

"Oh, jeez, I don't know," Lucas said. "I can't cook."

"Me either," Nina said. "Did you ever take home ec?"

"Nope. Did you?"

"Oh, yes, in the eighth grade. But the teacher broke her hip in the first week, and so they pulled Mr. Kaminsky up from the shop class to teach us."

"Why Mr. Kaminsky?"

"I don't know," Nina said. "I guess he had second hour free. It certainly wasn't because he knew anything about home economics. It was like being taught to cook by a man whose refrigerator was always empty except for a six-pack and an old potato."

Lucas laughed. "Did you learn anything at all?"

Nina glanced up at him in the moonlight. She smiled. "We used to make macaroni and cheese out of the box to an egg timer. It was all very complex and not very useful."

"Is that what you're going to bring? Macaroni and cheese?"

"Maybe . . ."

"We could make—"

"You could come over—"

They both fell silent at the same time. For a moment Lucas concentrated on the sound of Nina's nightgown rustling as she walked. He wanted more than anything to spend a fun hour whipping up some totally unsuitable dish in the Geigers' bright sunny kitchen while Nina laughed and teased him and did impersonations of Mr. Kaminsky. But things were still too awkward between them. And—it would feel like cheating on Zoey. Even though it wasn't, he reminded himself. Lucas guessed by Nina's expression that she was having the same thought.

"Nina," he said softly. "This is just what I didn't want to happen. We have to work through this."

She looked miserable. "How do we work through something so awful? How are we going to *work through it* with Zoey when she doesn't even know there's anything to work through? I worry about that enough *now*. How much do you think it's going to bother me when she's *here?* Then how am I going to handle the way I betrayed her?"

"*We* betrayed her," Lucas said. "But she never has to know, Nina. It would only hurt her."

"I know that!" Nina exploded. "Believe me, I'd be the last person in the universe who would ever tell her. But—but I don't want the burden of keeping a secret from her, either."

Lucas stared at her. Was she suggesting telling Zoey? "What do you mean?"

"I mean that I don't like our choices," Nina said. "I don't like the fact that it's either lie to Zoey or hurt her. I want to turn back the clock, and I can't do that."

Lucas said nothing. He knew she was right. He knew you couldn't turn back the clock, unring the bell, unkiss a girl, pretend years of your life weren't lost to a Youth Authority and a fishing boat. He struggled for a way to make Nina understand. "We'll just have to concentrate on how much we love Zoey," he said. "We have to forget that kiss ever happened—"

"How can I forget that kiss?" Nina whispered. "When it's all I can think about?"

Lucas might have thought she meant that in a romantic way except that she looked so exasperated, a small vertical line between her eyebrows, a tear glimmering in the corner of her eye like a single piece of glittery confetti.

Nina didn't like how she was feeling. She wanted to be feeling noble and honorable. But in reality she wanted Lucas to kiss her again. Not really, of course—she wouldn't hurt Zoey for anything. But Nina wanted to feel the way she felt that day on the beach. Safe. And cared for. Feelings she hadn't felt in a long time.

"I know how important Zoey is to you," Nina said.

"Nina, *you're* important to me," Lucas said, exasperated. Nina wished he would look at her, but all she could see was his profile. "We're both going to be here next year, and I don't want to spend the whole year thinking, *Gee, Nina and I could be having a great time if only I hadn't screwed things up.*"

"Oh," Nina said.

Lucas began walking again, and she hurried to keep up with him. Her bare feet were cold on the pavement. They were headed back toward her house. *Just like yesterday,* Nina thought. *He's going to be honorable and walk me home.*

Lucas was still talking, but Nina couldn't tell whether it was to her or to himself.

"We have to be friends," he said. "We're *going* to be friends. We're going to be friends if it—"

He was about to say if it kills us, Nina thought. *Or if it breaks my heart.*

Aisha

I feel like Christopher had an affair. That's how upset I am. I look back at our whole relationship, and it's all tainted by the fact that Christopher was married before and he didn't tell me.

Christopher was married before and he didn't tell me!

Why not tell me? It sure would've been simpler than all the trouble he went to in order to keep it from me. So why not just be honest. Unless

Unless he's still in love with her.

You can see why it's like he had an affair. It's worse than an affair in a way, because presumably if Christopher had an affair, he would beg my forgiveness. But he

144

doesn't seem to feel that's necessary. He doesn't seem to think he did anything even a teeny little bit wrong. And what does that say about Christopher?

For that matter, what does a seven-week marriage say about Christopher? Not really a sterling record. Why did they get divorced? Obviously they were young, maybe too young, but it's not like Christopher to give up on anything.

I wish I knew more about Carina. What was she like? What was it about her that made Christopher want to marry her? Was she like me? Does Christopher see something of Carina in me? Is that why he's so sure I was the girl for him right from the start?

I wish I could meet her. No matter how gorgeous, how intimidating, how tremendous she is in reality, she can't compare to the Carina I've created in my mind.

Seventeen

Kate had set her alarm for seven so she could take her medication, and instead of going back to bed she decided to write her mother a letter.

> Dear Mother,
>   Jake showed me the letter you wrote him and

Kate crumpled up the piece of paper. She was determined that this would be the last letter she ever wrote her mother. She didn't want it to be full of lies.

> Dear Mother,
>   I saw the letter you wrote Jake, and it has made several things clear to me, specifically, that I never want you to contact me again. No letters, no phone calls, certainly no visits. I am sure you will think this is another symptom of my

"denial," but it isn't. It is essential to my survival. I cannot have my attempts at recovery undermined by someone who sees depression as an "affliction" and not a treatable condition.

Please do not attempt to write Jake again, either, or try to involve him in any sort of scheme. He wasn't fooled by your letter and would only resent further attempts at manipulation.

I am confident that soon you will be too busy with your shopping and your friends to worry about someone you used to know.

Kate

Kate had folded the letter and put it in an envelope before she realized what she had written about Jake. *He wasn't fooled by your letter.* . . .

She knew it was true.

Nina had finally fallen asleep at seven in the morning, after rereading almost the whole Little House on the Prairie series and drinking multiple cups of hot cocoa. When the phone rang and woke her up at ten, *These Happy Golden Years* was face-down on her chest and her mouth tasted like an old Hershey bar.

"Hello?"

"Nina?" It was Zoey. "My mom gave me your new number. Did I wake you?"

"Yeah, but that's okay," Nina said. Her heart was racing.

"So why do you have a new number?"

"We've been getting all these crank calls; it's a long story. Listen, where are you?" Nina sat up in bed. "Are you home?" Was Zoey about to come over?

"No, I'm at one of my ten thousand stopovers," Zoey said. "Allegedly I'll get in about six this evening and be home at seven or so."

"Oh," Nina said.

"You still sound sleepy," Zoey said uncertainly. "I'm sorry I woke you, but I've been going stir-crazy on this train and—"

"Oh, it's okay," Nina said. "I'm glad you called."

For a moment the line hummed between them, and Nina had the crazy idea that Zoey would ask, Are you *really?* but of course she didn't.

"Have you seen Lucas?" Zoey asked instead.

Nina's mind raced. What should she say? What if she said no, and then later Zoey asked Lucas and he said yes? Or what if she said yes, and Lucas later said no? Or what if—

I'm not going to lie, Nina thought suddenly. *I'm not going to start lying to Zoey. Things are bad enough.*

"Yes, I saw him last night," she said.

"Oh, good, I was afraid he'd be lonely," Zoey said. Her voice was sincere, as clear and pure as water. "Where'd you guys go?"

"We—we didn't actually go anywhere," Nina said hesitantly. "I couldn't sleep and went for walk, and I happened to see Lucas. He couldn't sleep, either."

"What's wrong? Why couldn't you guys sleep?" Zoey said.

I should've just said we went for a walk, Nina thought.

"I guess he's just excited about you coming home," she said. "And I—I'm upset about Benjamin."

"Benjamin?" Zoey's voice echoed along the line. "What's he done now?"

Nina was startled for a moment before she remembered that she had never mailed the letter she wrote. "He didn't—I thought—we decided not to see each other anymore," she said falteringly.

"You broke up?"

"Well . . . yes. I mean, we both thought since—"

"That *idiot!*" Zoey exploded suddenly. "It's all because he feels like now he has to be Marco Polo, right?"

"Marco Polo?"

"Or Christopher Columbus or some other explorer. You know, all that business about how the world's out there waiting for him."

"Well, he couldn't do so much for all those years—"

"*Spare me!*" Zoey nearly screamed. "He met you, didn't he? He made someone wonderful fall in love with him. That's so much more than most people ever do, and now he acts like it's less important than—than—I can't even think of what; I'm too furious."

"Zoey—"

"Oh, no, and now I have to go," Zoey said. "Listen, we'll work this all out when I get home, okay? I miss you. Bye."

"Bye," Nina said, but Zoey was already gone.

Nina kept the phone next to her ear for a moment, ignoring the whine of the dial tone. She was thinking that she had been wrong, completely wrong, last night when she'd thought that Zoey would never take her seriously or be threatened by her.

Because if there was one person in the world who honestly thought highly of Nina, it was Zoey.

Aaron was in Luke's parents' garage, strapping a suitcase to the top of the van, when he heard a small voice say, "Hi, Aaron."

He turned around. It was Mia, wearing a pair of overall shorts over a pale green T-shirt. Her dark hair was pulled back in a green ribbon. She looked very young and very pretty.

"Hi, Mia," he said uneasily.

"Your mom told me you were leaving today," she said. "So I thought I'd come over and say good-bye."

Aaron wished his mother would keep her mouth shut. "Well, thanks," he said awkwardly. He occupied himself by tightening the luggage strap.

"Aaron?" Mia said in a small voice. "Was that girl really your girlfriend?"

Aaron hesitated. Then he shrugged. "She was."

"Oh." Mia was thoughtful for a minute. "Because someone told me that she was your stepsister."

Aaron smiled ruefully. "It's complicated."

"I guess." Mia apparently realized that he was going to keep working on the van. She sat down on an old cinder block. "Do you mind if I stay here for a minute?"

Aaron pushed another suitcase onto the top of the van. "If you like," he said. He threw a strap over the van and went around to the other side to secure it.

"Aaron?"

"Hmmm?"

"If that girl was your girlfriend, why did you go out with me?"

He had been dreading that question. How could he ever explain about his mother and the blind date and how he and Claire had agreed that they would only go out with other people once?

Mia was studying his face. "I mean, did you ever like me at all?"

Aaron could answer that one. "Yes," he said. "Yes, I did."

She smiled, a little bit sadly, and stood up. "I'd better get going," she said. She took a piece of paper out of her pocket and held it out to him. "That's my address. Will you write me?"

Aaron paused and then took the piece of paper. "Sure."

"Just, like, a postcard or whatever," she said.

"Okay."

"Well, bye."

"Bye."

She waited, and Aaron knew that she was hoping he would kiss her. He went back to work tightening the strap. After a second her footsteps trailed away.

He looked up when he heard a car stop at the end of the driveway. Claire was getting out of Burke's BMW. Aaron said a brief but heartfelt thanks to the God of Good Timing.

"Hi, Claire," he said as she walked up the drive. He waved to Burke as he drove off. "This is a surprise."

She shrugged. "I kind of surprised myself. I knew you were leaving, and my dad had an errand that would take him right by here. And I never mind taking a little jaunt to the mainland. So I thought—why not? Dad'll be back in a couple of minutes to pick me up."

Aaron wondered why she hadn't just driven herself so that she could stay as long as she wanted. Well, maybe that was the point, that she didn't want to stay. He didn't care. He was just happy to see her.

She was wearing jeans and a tight black T-shirt. He admired the way her dark hair waved back from her temples. "You look beautiful," he said. Then he glanced at her face sharply. "Beautiful but tired."

Claire looked away. "I haven't been sleeping well." She changed the subject. "So, all ready to go?"

Aaron nodded.

Claire looked at him and smiled gently.

Aaron wanted to hold her hand, but he didn't dare. "I'm packed," he said carefully. "But I don't like leaving you with things up in the air like this."

She crossed her arms, as though she had read his mind about wanting to hold her hand. "Well," she said, and paused. "I guess—"

One of the suitcases Aaron had put on top of the van fell off with a heavy thud. Aaron was startled, but Claire jumped and let out a small cry. Her hand flew to her throat. Aaron looked at the suitcase lying on the cement floor and then back at Claire. Her eyes were huge, and she turned so pale that Aaron led her over to the porch steps and helped her sit down. "I'm glad that didn't happen on the highway at seventy miles an hour," he said.

She didn't answer. A pulse showed itself in her

neck and beat there rapidly. "Claire, it's okay. Take it easy."

She seemed to pull herself together with an effort and gave him a shaky smile. "It was—" she said, but her voice was gone, and she had to clear her throat and start over. "It was right behind me," she said. "It surprised me."

"It sure did," Aaron said. He was relieved to see the color coming back into her cheeks.

Claire blew out her breath. "My dad's going to be here soon," she said, standing up.

"I meant what I said before," Aaron said. "I don't like leaving when things are—wrong between us."

Claire shrugged. "It's easier for me if you do leave while things are up in the air. I don't want to have to worry about what you're up to."

"Claire," he said. "I will never—"

"Quiet," she said, putting her hand over his mouth. As always, her touch was electric to him. "Let's not talk about it. Let's just say good-bye."

He pulled her into his arms and held her tightly, his lips buried in her hair. "Claire," he said softly. "I'll write you. And call."

"Thanks, Aaron. Have a good trip."

"Good-bye, Claire."

She walked down the drive and stood with her hand on the car door; she gave Aaron a half wave before she got in. Burke honked, and they drove away.

Aaron went back to loading the van. Claire had been in a strange mood: subdued. Aaron knew Claire better than most people. She had acted, well, *scared*.

Eighteen

Nina decided to make spinach dip for Zoey's party. She decided on spinach dip because Janelle agreed to walk her through it, step by step. However, Nina was so preoccupied thinking about Lucas that she had to ask Janelle to repeat everything at least once, and even then she left out the walnuts.

It was a very long hour for Janelle.

Lucas had decided to make lime Jell-O with mandarin oranges in it. But he opened a can of kidney beans by mistake. *Well, maybe nobody will notice the difference,* Lucas thought. In went the kidney beans.

Christopher made cherries jubilee. It was Aisha's favorite dessert.

Aisha didn't make anything. Her restless energy had deserted her. She looked at all the clothes she had emptied out of her bureau and closet and dumped on her bed. She wondered where she would sleep tonight.

Claire made a lemon soufflé. She did it the same way she did everything else: quickly, efficiently, expertly.

But when she was carrying the empty mixer bowl to the sink, a door slammed shut somewhere in the house and Claire jumped and the bowl fell out of her hands, breaking into a hundred jagged pieces—the approximate state of Claire's nerves.

Benjamin would have liked to make egg rolls or something interesting, but instead his mother made him roll silverware into napkins for so long that he had a *blister,* honest to God.

Kate bought flowers, which she said the Passmores could use as a centerpiece.

"Oh, my God," Lucas groaned. "Why didn't I think of that?"

Lara made brownies. She considered putting marijuana in them. But in the end, she settled for chocolate chips.

Nineteen

Kendra stood in the doorway of the B&B's business office. "Why aren't you going to Zoey's homecoming?"

"Because Christopher will be there," Aisha said. She opened one of the desk drawers and found a bottle of beige Liquid Paper.

"Why can't *I* go to Zoey's homecoming?" Kendra asked.

"Because you're coming with me." Aisha shook the bottle and then carefully dabbed some over the 1982 on her driver's license.

"Where are we going?" Kendra asked.

"Quiet, I'm concentrating." Aisha blew on the Liquid Paper to dry it and then rolled her driver's license into the typewriter. She aligned the carriage carefully and typed *1977*. She rolled it out and fit it carefully into the plastic casing in her wallet.

"*Where* are we going?" Kendra asked again.

"To a bar," Aisha said, putting the bottle away. "To get drunk."

Kendra beamed. "We are?"

Aisha reconsidered. "No, I am. You're going to have a Coke and tell me everything you know."

* * *

Claire was in her bedroom, wearing her underwear and trying to decide between two dresses. The dresses lay on her bed. They were both snug and flattering. One was sleeveless lime green, and the other was white with big red roses and cap sleeves. Normally Claire preferred the flowered dress, but today all those roses blooming on the white background reminded her of—well, of bloodstains.

I cannot go on being so morbid, Claire thought.

Resolutely she picked up the white dress and stepped into it, twisting her arms to zip up the back zipper. *There,* she thought, slightly out of breath. *He's not going to control what I* wear, *for heaven's sake.*

She went downstairs to the bathroom.

Nina was in there, wearing a raspberry-colored blouse and white miniskirt. She was applying raspberry-colored lipstick.

Claire stared at her. "You're wearing a *skirt?*"

"Shut up," Nina said, looking furious.

Claire saw that it wasn't actually a miniskirt; it was shorts with a flap across the front to make it look like a miniskirt.

"Will you stop staring at me, please?" Nina said irritably. "I was here first."

"I like it," Claire said.

"What?"

"I like it," she said again. "You look really great, really pretty."

Nina looked pleased for a moment, and then she frowned and her hand flew out to feel Claire's forehead. "Do you feel okay? Do you have a fever?"

"Oh, hilarious," Claire said. She stepped into the bathroom and rubbed a little styling gel between her palms. "Come here."

Nina looked suspicious. "Why? You look like you're about to wrestle me to the floor or something."

"Oh, give me a break," Claire said impatiently. She leaned forward and ran her hands through Nina's hair, gently tousling it. "Now look," she said, turning Nina to face the mirror. "Your bangs don't show so much this way."

Nina turned from side to side. "Hey, you're right," she said. She regarded her reflection critically.

She wants to looks pretty for Benjamin, Claire thought.

Nina met her eyes in the mirror. "I don't think you've ever *touched* me before," she said mischievously. "Are you sure you don't have food poisoning or something? Did you eat one of those hamburgers that Dad makes, with the meat practically still breathing?"

Claire rolled her eyes. "Get out of here," she said.

Nina laughed and flounced out of the bathroom.

Claire fixed her own hair and put on her makeup. But for once she wasn't satisfied with the way she looked, despite the hair that fell in rich waves to her shoulders and the full lips outlined in red lipstick and the sooty lashes—all the things that normally pleased her.

Her hand hovered over her makeup tray uncertainly. Finally she applied some more rouge to her pale cheeks and more concealer to the circles below her eyes. Claire had barely slept at all the night before.

When Zoey stepped off the train at the Weymouth station, she wanted to bend down and kiss the ground. *Good old Maine,* she thought. *I sure am happy to see you.*

"I'm sure Maine is happy to see you, too," her mother said from behind her. "I know I am."

Zoey laughed. "I didn't know I'd said that out loud."

Mrs. Passmore hugged her tightly. "Welcome home, sweetheart."

"It's nice to be home." She looked past her mother expectantly.

"If you're looking for Lucas, he's not here," her mother said.

Zoey tried to hide her disappointment. After all, she hadn't *asked* Lucas to come pick her up. She had just assumed he'd want to see her as soon as possible.

Her mother squeezed her arm. "You'll see Lucas sooner than you think," she said mysteriously. "But right now you'll have to make do with your boring old mom."

Zoey put her arm around her mother's waist. "I can make do with that just fine," she said.

But inside she wondered why she felt this need—this possessive, consuming need—to see Lucas and make sure she hadn't made a horrible mistake in leaving him.

Twenty

Lucas kept trying not to look at Nina, but it was like having a speck on your glasses: No matter where you look, you still see it. Nina was like that for him right now. A raspberry-colored blur in the corner of his vision, regardless of how hard he tried to concentrate on someone—anyone—else.

What Lucas actually wanted more than anything was to go talk to Nina. He wanted to take her away from that squirrely-looking guy she was talking to and lead her over to the sofa and sit there and talk to her all party long. But he didn't do it because he knew it would make him remember kissing her and then he would feel guilty and he didn't want to feel guilty at Zoey's homecoming.

So he didn't look at Nina.

Lara was sitting sulkily near the buffet, hating the dress she was wearing.

It was a pretty dress: soft black cotton with a sprinkling of tiny red and white flowers. Lara wore a small pearl choker to show off the neckline. She knew that the black was a good foil for her pale hair and that the cut of the dress showed off her small

161

waist. She knew she looked lovely and feminine, but she hated it.

The fact that Mr. Passmore had said, "Well, hey, look at you," about five times with genuine admiration in his voice had only made it worse.

Because this was the kind of dress that Zoey would wear. Lara realized now that she must have been thinking that on some level when she bought it. And that made her furious with herself—and with everyone who paid her a compliment. They should like her for herself, not as some pale imitation of Zoey.

She wondered why she had even come to this stupid party, where everything was centered around Zoey: loving mother dispatched to the station to pick her up, devoted father playing host, fond brother checking his watch, handsome boyfriend waiting with baited breath.

Lara let her gaze rest on Lucas. Life on the fishing boat certainly agreed with him. He looked more rugged and muscular than Lara remembered. What did a guy like him see in a mealymouthed goody-goody like Zoey? Lara wondered if he had a wandering eye. And, more to the point, would it wander Lara's way?

The idea of seducing Lucas away from Zoey was so sweet that Lara dimpled at her own thoughts.

"Hello, dear," an old lady said, approaching the buffet. "You look so sweet sitting there, smiling." She held out a soft old hand. "I'm Mrs. Harriman, Zoey's old piano teacher."

"I'm Lara," Lara said. She wondered briefly what Mrs. Harriman would say if she knew Lara was Mr. Passmore's illegitimate daughter. Could Lara possibly provoke a heart attack by telling her?

"Goodness, look at all this food," Mrs. Harriman said. "What shall I have first?"

Lara smiled again. "Have a brownie," she said. "I made them myself."

Well, this is typical, Nina thought. *This is just typical.*

Benjamin had winked at Nina and said, "Hi," when she had come in and then completely deserted her. Now he was splitting his time equally between Claire and Lara.

Aisha, who Nina had counted on to be her ally, hadn't even bothered to show, and Christopher was sitting in the corner, with his eyes trained on the door, watching for Aisha the way a dog waits for its owner to come back out of the store.

And Lucas was avoiding her like the plague. Nina couldn't seem to take her eyes off Lucas. She watched him talk to Mr. Passmore, slap Christopher on the back, say hello to Claire, say something in Benjamin's ear that made him laugh, bring Kate a glass of punch. But he didn't come near Nina. In fact, it seemed to her that he went to great pains to make sure he was on the opposite side of the room from her at all times.

Now Nina was cornered, talking to some nerdy friend of Mr. Passmore's who had a piece of spinach caught between his two front teeth. It was probably from Nina's own spinach dip.

"I'm a physics professor," the nerd was saying. "My students find me spellbinding. You ought to come sit in on a lecture."

"Yes, that certainly does sound like fun," Nina said, not bothering to hide her sarcasm. She ran her own tongue over her front teeth, hoping that he would take the hint. He didn't.

"Tuesday—" the nerd started but broke off as the room became quiet. Nina looked up.

Zoey had come home.

She stood in the doorway with Mrs. Passmore, surprised to see everyone there. She blinked at them, and suddenly all the guests screamed, "Welcome home!" and Zoey threw back her head and laughed. She moved into the room, accepting hugs and kisses, shaking hands, nodding, smiling.

She looked tired. Her makeup had rubbed off, and her soft dark blond hair was pushed behind her ears. There were delicate shadows below her blue eyes, and her clothes were limp on her body. *Even at her worst,* Nina thought, *Zoey is a thousand times more beautiful than I can ever hope to be.*

Zoey had reached Lucas. Everyone watched as he held out his arms to her. She stepped into his embrace. Nina watched it all as though in slow motion. Zoey's head nestled under Lucas's chin. He turned and rested his cheek on the top of her head. Her arms slipped around his neck. His hands met in the small of her back.

Nina hadn't understood before this how two people could fit together like pieces of a puzzle. She hadn't known that one person could *complete* another person, could supply something you hadn't even known was missing.

Twenty-one

The bartender barely glanced at Aisha's driver's license. "What'll you have?"

"Red wine," Aisha said recklessly. "Make it a double."

"Make it a what?"

"A double," she said, less certainly.

"What does that mean?" he asked. "You want two glasses or you want a double portion in a big glass or what? I never heard anyone order a double wine before."

"I want a double portion in a big glass," Aisha said meekly. She had only said that part about make it a double because she thought it would make her sound more sophisticated.

"Okay," the bartender said. He took a bottle of wine out from under the counter and began filling a big mug. "What do you want?" he said to Kendra. "A Shirley Temple?"

Kendra looked pleased. "Yes, thank you. With an extra maraschino cherry."

The bartender rolled his eyes and moved away to fix her drink. Aisha took a sip of her wine: acidic and sour smelling.

"So tell me more about Carina," she said to Kendra.

The bartender set Kendra's Shirley Temple down, and Kendra picked a maraschino cherry off the top. "I've already told you everything I know."

"You've told me two sentences," Aisha protested. "Tell me what she was *like*. Tell me how she and Christopher met, tell me if she laughed at your jokes, tell me if she had pierced ears, tell me what her favorite color was."

"I don't know her favorite color," Kendra said doubtfully.

Aisha rolled her eyes. "That was just an example," she said, exasperated. "Tell me *anything*."

"Okay, let me think," Kendra said, furrowing her brow. "Well, she wanted to be a lawyer."

"Good," Aisha said encouragingly.

"And . . . she knew how to make chocolate chip cookies that were superchewy. It had something to do with how much flour you add, but I can't remember now whether it was more or less. They sure were good, though. She would make them all the time, but she never ate any."

"Yes . . ."

"Well, that's about it, really. She didn't live with us long enough for me to get to know her very well. She was very friendly and open, though. I was really surprised when I found out about her later."

Aisha frowned. "Found out *what* about her?"

Kendra looked surprised, as though she thought Aisha would know. "Carina's a drug addict."

It seemed to Aisha that the room tilted dizzyingly. She tried to hold on to the bar stool, but her hands were like two blocks of wood. "A *what?*" she whispered.

"A drug addict," Kendra repeated. "Didn't Christopher tell you?"

Aisha's ears popped, and suddenly blood flowed back into her hands, making them tingle.

"Aisha?"

"No," Aisha said with an effort. "Christopher didn't tell me."

It seemed that there was a whole universe of things Christopher hadn't bothered to tell her.

"Was—was Christopher into drugs, too?" Aisha asked.

I can't believe I just asked that, she thought. *I can't believe I actually don't know the answer. But I don't.*

"You've got to be kidding," Kendra said. "Christopher? A drug addict? That's why he and Carina broke up—when he found out about her drug use."

Aisha was always surprised when people used the words *break up* instead of *divorce*. Didn't they know there was a difference? All the difference in the world.

"But Christopher must have known before they got married," she said. "You can't keep something like a steady drug habit a secret."

Kendra shrugged. "He just didn't know. I mean, it wasn't easy to tell. I never had a clue. She wasn't, like, always getting packages delivered or anything."

"What kind of drugs did she do?" Aisha asked.

Kendra shook her head. "I don't know. Christopher just came storming back about three weeks after they moved into their own place and said that Carina was a drug addict and that he'd given her an ultimatum, drugs or him. She chose drugs."

Aisha took a drink of her wine. A drug addict? It

seemed like that should explain part of the story, but it only made things more confused. Aisha wanted answers. She was beginning to feel like Christopher's marriage to Carina had been the most important, formative seven weeks of his life, and yet it was shrouded in mystery. Aisha didn't like mysteries. She liked everything out in the open, where she could evaluate the facts and make up her own mind.

But Kendra *couldn't* tell her what she wanted to know. Kendra was a third party. And Christopher *wouldn't* tell her. So how would she ever know what had really happened?

Aisha took another sip of her wine. It was terrible. What was she thinking? Drowning her sorrows wasn't *her*, wasn't her way. She was Aisha. She couldn't pretend to be some other kind of person.

She signaled the bartender. "Could I have a club soda?"

"What's wrong with your double?"

"Nothing," Aisha said firmly. "I just want a club soda—and wait." She dug in her purse. "Five dollars in quarters, please."

She gave four quarters to Kendra. "Go play some songs on the jukebox. We're going to be here a while."

Kendra sighed dramatically but moved off toward the jukebox.

Aisha was actually feeling better. She was going to stop feeling sorry for herself. She was going to take some action.

She walked over to the pay phone in the corner and dialed a number.

"Hello, Boston information. What area, please?"

"I'm afraid you're going to have to check the whole metropolitan area," Aisha said.

"What name, please?"

"Carina Connelly." She spelled it.

"I don't see a Carina Connelly listed, ma'am."

"How about C. Connelly, then?"

There was a brief pause. "I have fifty-six C. Connellys in greater Boston."

"I have paper and a pencil," Aisha said, digging around in her purse.

"Pardon?"

"I have paper and a pencil. Give me the numbers."

"All fifty-six?"

"Yes, please."

"Ma'am, that's a lot of numbers."

"That's okay," Aisha said. "I'm not going anywhere."

Lucas felt self-conscious hugging Zoey in front of a roomful of people. That is, he felt self-conscious until he had her in his arms. Then he just wanted to be alone with her.

Over the top of Zoey's head he saw Nina's face and felt guilty. He realized all at once that he was going to feel guilty from now on, no matter what he did.

"Hey, you look gorgeous, all covered with poppies," a voice said, and Claire turned around.

Benjamin was smiling at her.

She laughed. "They're *roses*." She went to sit next to him.

He frowned. "I thought they were poppies."

"Nope," Claire said, smiling.

Benjamin rubbed a corner of her dress between his thumb and finger. "Roses," he said softly, as though to himself.

"Benjamin," Claire said. "It's okay. It was still a nice compliment."

Benjamin didn't respond. He was still staring at a rose on the hem of her dress and rubbing his finger back and forth across it, as though trying to memorize it.

Why does it bother him so much? Claire wondered. *So he thought they were poppies. Big deal. Although it is a little weird . . . after all, he knows what a rose looks like, and I was only three feet away from him. Couldn't he see—*

But her thoughts were interrupted by Burke, who shook hands with Benjamin and said, "We haven't seen you around much."

Benjamin looked uncomfortable. "No, well, it's—it's been a busy summer."

"Well, don't be a stranger," Burke said, handing Claire a glass of punch and moving away.

Claire smiled sympathetically. "I'm afraid he's a little out of touch," she said.

He smiled wryly. "I imagine when the truth finally registers with him, I'll be a persona non grata at your house."

"Well, not if you drop Latin phrases," Claire said. "My dad loves that."

Something near the front door caught her attention. She thought she'd seen Aaron walk in, but it was Jake. Of course it wasn't Aaron. Aaron was off on his tour, and Claire wouldn't see him for weeks and weeks.

Claire shivered. A premonition, a sense of foreboding, touched her, and she knew without a doubt that this whole stalker business would be over by the time Aaron came home. One way or another.

Twenty-two

Lara watched Zoey and Lucas embrace and mentally deep-sixed the idea of seducing Lucas. She had to admit that he seemed pretty much in love.

This party was a drag. The most fun she'd had all night was giving Kate Levin scary looks from across the room. And now that Zoey was back, it was even more of a drag, watching everyone fall all over her.

Lara stood up and wondered idly where she'd left her purse. She glanced around the room and happened to see Lucas looking at Nina Geiger. On his face was a mixture of emotions much too complicated to read.

Lara's antennae—her psychic antennae—quivered. *What is that all about?* she wondered. She hesitated. Was it worth staying on the chance she might find out?

Something was definitely going on. She doubted it was any sort of infidelity, but a secret of some kind, nonetheless. Lara knew from experience that you could find out a lot just by keeping your eyes and ears open. And if she didn't find out tonight, she'd find out sooner or later. She was sure of it.

Lara sank back into her chair. She felt downright cheerful.

* * *

Zoey was almost to Nina. Nina watched her come.

"Professor Merton!" Zoey exclaimed gaily to the nerd, squeezing his arm. And then she was hugging Nina.

"Oh, God," Zoey whispered. "Calgon, take me away."

"You're doing beautifully," Nina whispered back. She smelled Zoey's shampoo, her perfume, her sweat, her skin. *Lucas has smelled all this, too,* she thought.

"I never thought I'd say this." Zoey was still whispering. "But—*I'm tired of talking about myself!* If one more person asks me how Washington was, I'm going to have a nervous breakdown."

"Oh, well . . ." Nina couldn't think of what to say.

"Zoey," Mrs. Passmore called.

"Oh, God." Zoey groaned, breaking away. "Duty calls. Hang around, though, okay? I *do* want to talk to you." And she went obediently on to the next person.

The nerd closed in on Nina again. "So, as I was saying, Tuesdays I have class from . . ."

A few feet away Lucas had taken Zoey's arm. She smiled up at him. He said something, and she shook her head.

". . . This week is going to be especially thrilling," the nerd was saying. "We're starting thermodynamics."

Nina looked at him with ill-concealed irritation. If only he would shut up, she might be able to hear what Lucas was saying. *Oh, why torture yourself?* she thought.

"Excuse me," she said to the nerd. "I'm going to the bathroom."

"Well, hurry back," the nerd said, waggling his eyebrows at her.

Oh, for God's sake, Nina thought disgustedly.

She slipped through the crowd and up to the bathroom on the first-floor landing. She closed the door and leaned against it. This whole scene was a nightmare. She should never have come. She should have invented some excuse. She splashed cold water on her face and fished a Lucky Strike out of her purse. She put it in her mouth, but she was so tense that she bit it and tasted tobacco. Grimacing, she threw it in the wastebasket. She opened the door. She would go say good-bye and escape. Maybe—

She froze.

She heard voices coming from above her. From the landing outside Zoey's room.

"Come *in* here," Zoey said coaxingly.

"Zoey," Lucas said. "I am not going into your room with you while there's a priest in the house."

Zoey laughed. "He's not a priest, he's a minister."

"Whatever. I'm still not going," Lucas said, but Nina could hear the smile in his voice.

Nina didn't stay to listen. She hurried down the stairs, but not fast enough. She heard the door to Zoey's room shut. She closed her eyes and thought about how strong Lucas was, how wiry and well built. She thought about how slight Zoey was. Zoey couldn't force Lucas to do anything he really didn't want to do.

Zoey pulled Lucas into her room and shut the door. "Come on, I just want to change."

"Oh, great," Lucas said. "That's going to look wonderful—we go upstairs together, and you come down wearing something different."

"Don't be paranoid," Zoey said, kissing him. She couldn't stop touching him, kissing him, hugging him.

Someone, Benjamin, probably, had brought up her luggage, and Zoey went quickly to her suitcase and opened it. She shook out a sleeveless cream-colored linen sheath. "Turn around," she said, unbuttoning her blouse.

Lucas hesitated.

"Go on," she said. "You're the one uncomfortable with having sexy thoughts while there's a minister in the house."

Lucas turned around. "Yeah, well, there I am, hugging you in front of everyone, and I turn around and this man says, *Hello, I'm Pastor Evans.* It was disturbing."

Zoey laughed and peeled off her jeans. "I wish I had time for a shower," she said, stepping into her dress. "I feel like—like I don't know what."

"A person who's been on a train for two days?" Lucas suggested.

"Yes, exactly!" Zoey said. "You can turn around now."

She dug around in her suitcase and pulled out a headband of tiny artificial daisies. The daisies were exactly the same color as her dress. She pushed the headband into her hair and frowned. "What do you think?"

She could see Lucas watching her in the mirror. "I like it."

"You're sure?" she said, facing him. "It's not too—too *Midsummer Night's Dream* or anything?"

"No," Lucas said with the same lopsided grin that still made her heart skip a beat. "You look beautiful."

She crossed the room and put her arms around him. "I'm glad you think so," she said softly. She kissed him. "I'm sorry I went away."

Lucas's eyes were troubled. "Zoey, so much happened while you were gone, and none of it good. I—"

"Let's talk later," she said, kissing his jaw. "I want to do something else now."

"Zoey—"

But she was insistent, covering his face with small kisses, pressing her body against his, and soon he was kissing her back, with growing urgency. Zoey held on to him and felt the familiar excitement.

Whatever's wrong, I'll fix it, she thought. Lucas pulled her against him, and she felt so confident and happy, she thought that every cell of her body must be in perfect alignment.

Twenty-three

Aisha was on the twenty-first C. Connelly. Her voice was hoarse. She had drunk her club soda and even her wine, but she had never been less tipsy in her life.

This is hopeless, Aisha thought. *Carina probably doesn't even live in Boston anymore. Or if she does, she's married, or changed her name, or has an unlisted phone number. I should've asked for Carina Shupe. Well, if none of these is her, I'll call information again.*

She dialed the twenty-first number and leaned against the wall.

"Hello?" A man's voice.

"Could I speak to Carina?" Aisha said.

"I think you have the wrong number," the man said.

"Sorry, I must have mis—" Aisha said, but he'd already hung up. She shook her head tiredly and dialed the twenty-second number.

"Hello?" It was a girl's voice, throaty and friendly sounding.

"Hello," Aisha said. "I'm looking for Carina Connelly."

"Just a minute," the girl said.

"I already picked up," another voice said easily.

This voice was quick, light, sweet. "This is Carina," the voice said. "Who am I speaking to?"

Lucas edged Zoey back toward the bed. Her knees hit the edge of the mattress, and suddenly she stopped kissing him and said, "Wait! My dress will get wrinkled."

Lucas groaned. "You're not worried about eternal damnation by Pastor Evans, but you don't want your dress to get wrinkled?"

Zoey straightened her headband. "That about sums it up," she said cheerfully. She took his hand. "Besides, someone will send out a search party soon if we don't get back."

Lucas sighed.

"Hey," Zoey said, taking his chin and forcing him to look at her. "We'll have plenty of time later."

Her eyes held promises, and Lucas thought, with a sinking heart, how happy he would be if she weren't going away.

Or if she'd never gone.

He ran a hand through his hair. "Okay, let's go downstairs," he said. "We can see if anyone's eaten a piece of my Jell-O yet."

"Oh, is that your Jell-O?" Zoey asked. "The one with the pieces of liver floating in it?"

Of course, Nina couldn't just *leave*. She had to say good-bye to Mrs. and Mr. Passmore. She had to listen to Burke say that Claire had already left, pleading a headache, and he hoped both of them weren't coming down with something. She had to disentangle herself from the nerd.

And all the while Nina replayed the sound of that door shutting in her mind.

Finally she gave her last tremulous, false smile, said her last, "Yes, thank you, I'm sure I'll feel better," and she was out the Passmores' back door, standing in the cool of their patio.

"Nina? Don't leave."

Oh, God, who now? Nina thought wearily. Her shoulders slumped. She turned.

It was Lucas.

"Don't go," he said softly. "Zoey wants you to stay. She's dying to see you."

I don't care what Zoey wants, Nina thought sullenly. *Zoey already has everything she wants.*

That was uncalled for, another voice in her mind whispered. *What are you—jealous?*

Shut up! Nina told the voice savagely.

But the voice wouldn't be silenced. *What are you—jealous?* it asked over and over. *What are you—jealous?*

What if I am? Nina thought. *What if, for once in my life, I want to be the romantic lead and not the comic relief?*

Lucas was looking at her strangely.

"Tell her—tell her I don't feel good," Nina managed at last.

Lucas came out onto the patio. He studied Nina's face and then took her hand and pulled her over by the forsythia bushes, where they weren't in direct sight of the party anymore. "What's wrong?"

Anger boiled up in Nina. "Oh, nothing," she said acidly. "Everything's wonderful."

Lucas looked taken aback. "What did I do?"

"Nothing!" Nina flared at him. "You did absolutely nothing! You go on and on about how you don't want us to avoid each other, and then what do you do? You act like I'm invisible!"

Lucas opened his mouth to speak, but Nina cut him off.

"I *saw* you," she said, fury making her voice waver. "I sat there and I saw you being all lounge lizardy—"

"Lounge—"

"All slick and charming, with everyone but me! You couldn't even say hello to me! You couldn't even rescue me from that horrid little math guy! You acted like—" She faltered. She felt a tear on her cheek.

Oh, great, she thought. *Now I'm going to cry.*

Lucas put his arms around her. "Nina, I'm sorry," he said softly. "Please. You have every right to be mad, but please don't. I don't think I could stand it at this point."

Nina bowed her head inside the safe circle of his arms. She wiped her eyes. How nice it was to have him near her again. How soothing—

"Lucas? Nina?" Nina blinked and looked toward the back door. Zoey stood there, a puzzled smile on her face. "What are you guys doing?"

Claire unlocked the front door and stepped inside, carefully locking it behind her. Her sleepless night had caught up with her at the party, and she felt drained and exhausted. She'd walked home with the Shaws, who lived just up the street.

Claire's hair and dress smelled of potato chips and pastrami and punch. She wanted to take a long, hot shower and drop into bed. It was still daylight. She could take a long nap, which would ruin her sleep tonight, but Claire suspected that she probably wouldn't do much sleeping tonight, nap or no nap.

She went upstairs to her room and stripped off her

dress. She saw the lime green dress crumpled on the floor, but she was too tired to pick it up. She put on a robe and walked down the stairs and took a shower.

Five minutes later she was back in her room, toweling her hair dry. She threw the towel on a chair and walked over to her dresser for a nightgown. She pulled open the bottom drawer, barely glancing in, and drew out an old yellow cotton gown. She shook it out absently and then stared at it, numb.

The gown had been slashed.

Claire's mind was frozen. She could see the long, ragged cuts, and her finger could feel the shredded fabric, but she couldn't understand it. She dropped the yellow gown and took another one out of the drawer. It was slashed, too.

Moving more quickly now, she emptied the drawer. Every gown was in ribbons. She stood up and crossed the room to her closet. The door was open, and she could see the long flaps of fabric. She began pulling things out at random: blouses, skirts, dresses. All slashed, all cut.

She whirled and picked the lime green dress off the floor. It was in pieces.

Someone had been here, here in her house, here in her bedroom, in just the past hour. Someone had taken a knife and slashed her clothes with vicious, angry strokes, as though venting some boundless rage. Someone had stabbed her clothes with horribly vivid symbolism. He had been angry that she wasn't here, he had hoped she would be here, he had wanted Claire to be in these clothes when he sliced into them—

Claire fainted.

Making Out: Lara Gets Lucky

**Book 23 in the explosive series about
broken hearts, secrets, friendship,
and of course, love.**

Lara's out to hurt **Zoey.** What better
way than to catch **Lucas** and **Nina**
together? **Nina** misses **Ben,** and
Lucas fears losing **Zoey,** so they need
each other. But then **Lara** sees something
that will upset **Zoey** for sure. There's
trouble for everyone when . . .

Lara gets lucky

READ ONE…READ THEM ALL—
The Hot New Series about Falling in Love

MAKING OUT

by KATHERINE APPLEGATE

MAKING OUT

by KATHERINE APPLEGATE

Love stories just a little more perfect than real life...

Don't miss any in the
enchanted ♥HEARTS
series: